"Hey, you—hey, wait up a sec!" called out Andy as he, the Ironman, and the Spider lumbered briskly toward Stephan. Stephan gave a half turn, just enough to catch sight of who was calling to him, but instead of stopping, if anything he quickened his pace. "You know, that's not very nice," said Andy, galloping up with his posse. "Hey, don't you know I kind of thought you were more friendly than that. After all, you did come to my church for Christmas services. So how come you came to my church?"

"I've got to get back to work now," Stephan explained, as Andy and the Ironman, who could double as a human wall, barred his way while the Spider sandwiched him in from behind as though he were nothing more than a piece of luncheon meat haphazardly thrown between a couple of slices of bread. "Look, I've got to go," Stephan pleaded. "I'm already late."

"Now, now, you don't have to be like that 'cause I just want to introduce you to my friends."

Other Bantam Starfire Books you will enjoy

THE YEAR WITHOUT MICHAEL
  by Susan Beth Pfeffer

THE FACE ON THE MILK CARTON
  by Caroline B. Cooney

DESPERATE PURSUIT by Gloria D. Miklowitz

LANDING ON MARVIN GARDENS
  by Rona S. Zable

FORBIDDEN CITY by William Bell

FIRE MASK by Charles L. Grant

SPLIT IMAGE by Michael French

WAITING FOR THE RAIN by Sheila Gordon

The Drowning of Stephan Jones

by Bette Greene

BANTAM BOOKS
NEW YORK · TORONTO · LONDON · SYDNEY · AUCKLAND

Though this novel was inspired by a real drowning, it is a work of fiction. All of the characters in the book, whether central or peripheral, are purely products of the author's imagination, as are their actions, motivations, thoughts, and conversations. Neither the characters nor the situations which were created by the author are intended to depict real people or real events.

THE DROWNING OF STEPHAN JONES
A Bantam Book

PUBLISHING HISTORY
Bantam hardcover edition / November 1991
Bantam paperback edition / November 1992

The Starfire logo is a registered trademark of Bantam Books,
a division of Bantam Doubleday Dell Publishing Group, Inc.
Registered in U.S. Patent and Trademark Office and elsewhere.

ISBN 0-553-29793-7

Published simultaneously in the United States and Canada

Bantam Books are published by Bantam Books, a division of Bantam Doubleday Dell Publishing Group, Inc. Its trademark, consisting of the words "Bantam Books" and the portrayal of a rooster, is Registered in U.S. Patent and Trademark Office and in other countries. Marca Registrada. Bantam Books, 666 Fifth Avenue, New York, New York 10103.

PRINTED IN THE UNITED STATES OF AMERICA

OPM   0 9 8 7 6 5 4 3 2 1

Acknowledgments

There were many people who took the time and trouble to share their insights with me during the writing of this book. There are two people that I must thank first and foremost: my great editor at Bantam Books, Beverly Horowitz, because she embraced a book that frightened lesser souls, and second, but not really second, I need to thank my best friend and husband, Donald Sumner Greene.

The honored and appreciated others are: Nita Bernard, Massachusetts Gay and Lesbian Political Caucas, Chief Butch Esty, Herbert and Sylvia Evensky, Attorney Lauren Field, Attorney Marvin Himmelfarb, Phoebe Wall Howard, Diana Ajjan, Carla Greene, Billy Greene, Jordan Greene, Christy Johnson, Rabbi Ira Korninow, Rabbi Barry Krieger, Attorney William Kunstler, Carolyn A. Markuson, Attorney Andrew B. Myers, Episcopal Divinity School, Stanley Stallons, Professor Wendell W. Watters, Susan Arnsby of People for the American Way, Charles White, Gary Keegan, Fundamentalists Anonymous, Reverend Pat Carroll, Reverend Gary Smith, D. J. Corvin, Southern Poverty Law Center, National Gay and Lesbian Task Force, Weston School of Theology, Nora Barton Bryant, Joseph Walsh, Archdiocese of Boston, Dorothy F. Green, Lois Reed, Renee Golden, Alison Clarick, Jeanette and Tom Hackett, Gretchen O'Brien, the Broilerhouse Restaurant, Bangor Public Library, Mary Ann Nelson, Reta Schrieber, Joe Roy, Harry F. Gordon, Sandy and Ken King, Professor David Hershenson, Marion Hershenson, Jan Meins, Kevin Berrill, Cheryl Cutler, Brookline Public Library, Peterborough Public Library, Judge Jim Lair, Attorney William E. Strickland, Jr., Pat Matsukis, King Gladden, Jean Elderwind, Reverend Sally Williams-Gorrell, Bill and Iris Simantel, Mary Jane Sheard, Cindy Todd, Richard Schoeninger, The Women's Project of Little Rock.

If there is anyone whose help I have forgotten to acknowledge, I certainly apologize for the oversight.

Chapter 1

CARLA WAYLAND HAD every intention of entering Harris's Handy Hardware Store just as though she were the world's greatest actress triumphantly striding across the spotlit stage to embrace her Oscar. But by the time she reached Jerry's TV Sales and Service two doors west of the hardware store, her heart was rat-a-tat-tatting against the walls of her chest. To distract herself from what felt like a fatal case of nervousness, she stopped and stared at the enormous fifty-two inch color TV in Jerry's window.

Although the volume was turned low, she was startled by the nearly life-sized images of men and women marching and waving cardboard signs, pink triangles on a solid black background. In front of the state capitol in Little Rock, their briskly waving banners demanded: GIVE US OUR RIGHTS! and PASS GAY RIGHTS NOW!

Suddenly the camera panned to an opposing group of angry people, many of whom looked as though their faces had been left to harden in cement. Several hundred strong they marched waving the twin banners of the Moral Majority and the Christian Decency League. In the bone chilling cold, they chanted: "Hay-hay! HI-HO . . . All the queers have got to GO. . . . Hay-hay! HI-HO . . . All the queers have got to GO . . ."

The camera seemed to fixate on these people who were heckling the gay rights protesters. Carla was struck as much by their hands jabbing into the air as by their granite looks misshapen by hatred. Fists clenched, they screamed "SAVE OUR CHILDREN! STOP THE QUEERS! SAVE OUR CHILDREN! STOP THE QUEERS! . . ."

Although some of the placards looked professionally printed, the largest one carried a message clumsily written with a Magic Marker on a grayish-white sheet:

THE SILENT MAJORITY SAYS NO!
NO RIGHTS BUT DEATH RIGHT
FOR
PORNOGRAPHERS-MOLESTERS-FAGS!!!

Instead of being calmed down, Carla felt agitated. Why, she then wondered, was she getting herself worked up over this? This wasn't her battle! She certainly wasn't gay, and she didn't even know anybody who was. Was it only because she always managed to feel sympathetic for anyone who was being picked on? Particularly people who were picked on because they were different? Being different, boy, could she ever understand that!

That news segment ended, and an anchorwoman on the nightly news began asking the handsome young governor of Arkansas for his comments on whether or not he would run for the office of president of the United States. Carla turned from the screen and quickly began walking again toward Harris's. She reminded herself that she was not about to become unstrung over some injustice happening over in the state capitol. Lord knows, there was injustice aplenty in her own little northwest corner of Arkansas, right in good ol' Rachetville, U.S.A.

Besides, she was about to do something for *herself,* something that would stop the hurt of loving someone who didn't know that she existed. Oh, sure—he knew her name and face all right, he probably always had, but he didn't *know* her, not a bit. She was hellbent on making certain that that would soon change!

Even before reaching her destination, Carla was busy telling herself how much steadier and calmer she felt. And as she fished her lipstick and compact from her purse, it became necessary to wipe her perspiring palms against both sleeves of her navy duffle coat. It came as a surprise that her hands were so hot and sticky, because this particular late-December day was about as cold as it ever got in this town.

Carla cooled and calmed herself down with her very own whispered words of encouragement: "Probably a hundred—probably even more than a hundred—people pass through these doors daily, especially now, only three days till Christmas, so why in the world would anybody think twice about one more person—namely me—doing the same exact thing?"

As she brought the tube of Crimson Nights to her lips a man speaking mere inches from her ear softly whispered, "Somebody's going to be impressed." Carla was startled. The words as well as the warm

3

sound of the cultured accent and well-modulated voice suggested that he had come from someplace a long way from this place, and both gave her more courage.

Carla had never really lived any place else or even been very far from her Ozark Mountain home. Even so, there just seemed to be something within her that always made her yearn for experiences she had never had as well as places, far-far-away places, where she had never been. Although she mightily resisted looking up, she felt as though she just had to put a face on that wondrous voice. She looked up.

Without slowing his step, the man flashed a slightly sideways conspiratorial smile. And as he and his equally good-looking male companion entered the store, Carla stood statue-still. Despite the cold, she somehow felt warmed as well as encouraged. Actually she felt as though the stranger was at this precise moment a friend. As she slid the lipstick across her heart-shaped lips, she wondered if friendships had to endure for a certain period of time before they could actually qualify as friendships?

Carla breathed the mountain air deeply before throwing her chin up, squaring her shoulders, crossing all of her fingers, and entering the well-lit hardware store. Once inside, she looked neither to the left nor to the right but headed purposefully for the Christmas light display. At first the only Mr. Harris she sighted was Andy's father, the proprietor. Mr. Lawrence Harris had a reputation in town of knowing practically everything there was to know about hardware, and there weren't many do-it-yourselfers who hadn't at one time or other profited from his constructive advice. Harris's Handy Hardware Store's housewares catalog went out several times a year all over this state, and in Oklahoma and Tennessee, too.

Plenty of mail-order money flowed into the pockets of Mr. Harris. It also flowed *out* of those very same pockets; you could just tell by the way that both the father and the son dressed that their clothes were bought through the catalogs of stores that purported to have come into this world to cater only to sportsmen and gentlemen.

What always struck Carla about Mr. Harris was the way he seemed to take such commanding control of his cash register. It reminded her of the way a combat pilot might take charge of his cockpit. At this moment, however, Mr. Harris was lazing against the counter of his television department as he watched one of the several turned-on sets that brought the six o'clock news from Little Rock.

Although Carla kept her head down, pretending to stare transfixed at the festive display of Christmas ornaments and lights, her searching eyes were still able to catch an occasional discreet, passing glimpse of Andy, who was deeply engrossed in demonstrating a microwave oven. It was clear, at least to Carla, that this lady customer was unaccustomed to hearing such strong and persuasive salesmanship flowing so smoothly from a mere lad of seventeen. Andy was wearing a baby-blue sweater that looked positively washed-out faded when compared to the truer blue of his eyes. Carla was convinced that with those extraordinary eyes there wasn't anything he couldn't sell.

When Carla rhapsodized about those eyes to her best friend Debby, she could almost make her believe that Andrew Anthony Harris's blues were truly one of the really wondrous wonders of the Western world.

Carla couldn't tell for certain, but she would have bet a buck that her hero was wearing matching socks. He had a reputation to uphold of being a sharp dresser.

Although Carla absolutely, positively knew for a fact that Andy couldn't tell she was observing him, she was terrified that somehow he might just up and guess that she was, so she purposely refocused her eyes on the man with black hair who had whispered encouragement to her. A wool scarf of bright scarlet tossed across the stranger's neck gave him a casually elegant air, and for some reason she felt it also gave him a decidedly brave look.

Brave? Carla came pretty close to laughing aloud. She recognized the laughter part as definitely her mother's influence. Sometimes she wondered if Judith, who had taught her to question everything, had perhaps taught her a little too well. But then again, on second thought, maybe just maybe she was right the first time, because it really was true that no man in Rachetville would ever be brave enough to be caught dead wearing a scarf, leastways not a flaming red one!

If an out-of-towner were to drive through downtown and glance around at what the menfolk were wearing, then he'd quickly come to the conclusion that folks don't give one god damn about what they throw on their bodies. But boy oh boy, would he ever be wrong! And if that same stranger got the impression that there's not a dress code in all of Rachetville, well then, he'd sure enough be wrong again. 'Cause the rule, the never-to-be-broken rule, was and always would be: Clothes have to be rough and tough to show the world who the wearer was and always would be even more rough and tough.

The red-scarfed stranger was as far removed from

the Rachetville dress code as you could get. And if that wasn't enough then there was still another thing that fascinated her, the vertical line that ever-so-decisively bisected his forehead like an exclamation point. It was clear to Carla that his energies were now focused on convincing his blond-haired companion of something terribly important about one of those small appliances.

Chapter 2

IT WAS A cinch to see that the two obviously intense men over at the small-appliance counter were disagreeing with each other and actually beginning to lose patience with one another. "Money be damned!" her dark-haired "friend" burst out, loud enough to be heard clearly even at this distance. His startled companion, whose light-as-beaten-eggwhite skin was stretched tight enough over his high cheekbones to make any Apache wince with envy, gave his friend little patty-pat-pat signs, trying to calm him down.

And he did calm down, too, but not before that overheard phrase had piqued the interest of the unseen matron who'd been listening to Andy from the next aisle over. Her beautifully coiffed salt-and-pepper-colored head began to visibly turn so she could better overhear the man who spoke with so passionate a voice. "Why, dammit, *why* is it so hard for you to understand? I hate not being able to buy you beautiful things, fast cars, or go on trips to romantic places. Well, by God, I can at least buy you the best damn ice-cream maker in this town. And that's little enough to do for you . . . my love!"

At this point, the listening lady seemed to have forgotten all about her handsome salesman, for on her lips was just the barest trace of a smile. It was as though she had become wistful, almost girlish, as she was flooded with memories of a time past when she was young . . . and in love.

However, her reveries were shaken and then shattered as two men appeared with the ice-cream maker. Holding the chosen appliance aloft, Frank Montgomery, the man who had mere minutes ago encouraged Carla, inquired, "Sorry to intrude, but would you know if you have another just like this one? Only still in the box?"

Andy dropped obediently to his knees to search on the lowest shelf for the sought-after appliance, while the woman's eyes protruded as she stared unblinkingly at the two men. First she shook her head one way and then she shook her head the other way. In the same kind of a way you might shake away a nasty little mosquito . . . or maybe an even nastier little truth!

Slowly it dawned on her that there was no other possible explanation except *that* explanation. And no other truth except *that* truth! The same, exact truth that was right now banging up her senses. Sucking in great quantities of air, she seemed to grow boxier and more bosomy. As quickly and as deadly as a cobra, hissing reptilelike at the startled men, she spat out a lone, venomous word: *"Sodomites!"*

Instantly, silence fell throughout the store. Not a

normal silence, but more like an end-of-the-world-as-we-know-it silence. There didn't seem to be a single eye that wasn't now staring at the men who stood publicly condemned.

The deep olive of her "friend's" complexion seemed to turn two shades darker, while the other, light-haired man's already pale skin became completely chalky. It was clear to Carla that the pale man was going to bolt. And that's probably what would have happened, too, if her friend hadn't reached out his hand and placed a sustaining but gentle touch on his forearm. Frank wordlessly told Stephan that there was not all that much to be afraid of. At least not more than they were capable of facing together.

Like a man who has had more experience with emotional self-defense than he ever wanted, Frank Montgomery sighed wearily. "Know something, madam?" He spoke clearly, allowing his quizzical voice to ring out strong and proud. "You remind me of something my mother once taught me. A long time ago, she sat me down and said, 'Frankie, I know you'll forget a lot of what I tell you, but I sure hope that you'll always remember this: Only a real honest-to-goodness *pervert*,"—he twisted the last word so hard that it seemed to come out of his mouth harshly deformed—"would get jollies worrying about other people, and exactly what it is they do or *don't* do behind closed doors!"

The woman's eyes widened still further and her lipstick-bright mouth hung slack. She looked exactly the way a woman would look who, without warning or cause, had been slapped violently across her face. She panted audibly for air while the moments dragged on endlessly, as though time had in some way become stuck in a long-forgotten time warp. Then the moment passed. Still breathing hard, she abruptly turned to almost hurl her hefty body toward the door.

Before exiting, she twirled on sensible heels to give the men a final piece of her mind. "If you for one minute think that our God-fearing Christian legislators are going to pass *your* gay rights . . ." she boomed out. All background noises ceased and Carla and all the other startled customers and clerks continued to stare. "Well, let me tell you this: You've got another thing a-coming! Just because you faggots are ranting and raving and carrying on about your rights outside our statehouse—who do you think you are? If God wanted you to have rights, then why would he have gone and invented AIDS!?" Then, without waiting even a millisecond for any possible response, she flung herself out the door.

The store was so still and the people in it so shocked silent that the scene looked like a photograph. The moment was interrupted by Frank Montgomery's cool and calm voice. "Oh, you've located one!" he said, sounding very pleased as he noticed a physically and emotionally stalled Andy holding a box with a full-color picture of the wanted appliance on the outside of the carton. "Would you be a good fellow and gift-wrap it, please?"

Andy stammered and nodded his head at least two or three times more than what was actually necessary. But after placing the boxed item on the counter next to his father's beloved cash register, the boy kind of backed himself away, leaving the two strangers to face his father. At first, Carla was puzzled; she couldn't exactly make sense of it. With all those eyes, all those angry eyes, fixed on them, why did both of the men seem so deliberate in their motions, as though they had all the time in the world? Wouldn't you think that they'd stare down at the floor while practically racing out just as fast as their feet could carry them?

But the more she observed, the more the answer became apparent: They wouldn't want—couldn't accept— for the onlookers to think that they could be so easily scared away like a pair of dumb animals in the night.

With his arms folded defiantly across his drum barrel of a chest, Lawrence Harris glared down at the boxed appliance as though his own ice-cream machine had been transformed before his eyes into a toxic dump site. Pretending not to notice the merchant's fixed face of fury, Frank pointed to a festive roll of green-and-red Santa Claus wrapping paper beneath the counter. Slipping some bills from his wallet, he asked pleasantly, "Would you please wrap it with the Christmas paper? It's a gift."

Lawrence Harris made change, then picked up the unwrapped cardboard box, tore off a short piece of gift paper, and placed the items on the counter into Frank's less-than-willing hands. "You've got what you came for," he said, his words emerging heavily encrusted with contempt. "Now get the hell out of here!"

Even from this distance Carla noticed that the strong jaw lines of both Frank and Stephan had become set, harder and more prominent. "I see you eagerly took my money. I *will* take my purchase and I *will* leave," Frank said evenly. "But before I do I'd like to ask you something."

"Ask away, fruit fly!"

Frank looked him straight in the eye and made a series of small nods of the head. "Who was it that taught you to hate? Who was it that so carefully and so painstakingly taught you to hate?"

Lawrence Harris's face burst flame-red. "Why YOU—YOU!—" Even as he began sputtering, Frank turned smartly on his heels and he and Stephan strode energetically—but without any noticeable haste—out the door. The enraged proprietor watched the door open and close behind them. When some of the red began to fade from his face, he declared arrogantly, "Somebody with a little guts would do the whole world a favor if they'd blow both of those fags' brains to smithereens!"

From the far side of the store, his son thoughtfully took in his dad's words. Removing his hand from the pocket of his chinos, he fashioned a pretend gun with his right hand, closed one blue eye as though taking deadly aim through a gunsight, and to nobody in particular, announced with an air of finality, "Bang! You're dead! And bang! You're dead, too."

Chapter 3

THE PACE OF Harris's Handy Hardware Store was returning to something that might pass for normal, but Carla didn't feel one bit normal. Her emotions were spinning faster than last April's cyclone, the one that whipped the roof right off Clyde Thompson's video store.

There were slivers of a moment here and slivers of a moment there when she was dead certain she felt one thing, but the very next instant, she'd be equally convinced that what she was feeling was the exact opposite! Like, for example, when she was sure that she felt blind rage that her "friend" deceived her by acting supremely masculine, but *wasn't*. But in the next tidbit of an instant, she thought that, except for this weird notion of his to love one of his own sex, maybe he was just as much a male as any other guy. Male? Female? Don't you have to be one thing or the other? If you're not one thing then don't you definitely have to be the other? At this point, the only thing that she was convinced of was her own confusion.

She was sure of sadness at the way the men had been publicly ridiculed. Why, oh why would the lady and Mr. Harris want to talk that ugly way to living, breathing human beings? Did they only feel big by making others feel small? Or were they blinded by their own self-righteousness?

There was something else engraved on her heart, and that was a sense of disappointment in herself. Somehow, out in the cold in front of the hardware store he had recognized her trepidation. He'd risked rejection to whisper encouragement in her ear. He had come to her rescue when she was alone. But she hadn't come to his. Why hadn't she done something, said anything, to help them? One thing she knew for sure—she was completely unworthy of being called Judith Wayland's daughter. But she wasn't involved, so what could she really do? But Carla knew her mother would never have to ask that question. Judith seemed to have come into this world knowing exactly what she should do and why she should do it. No, Judith Wayland would never sit on her hands, or on her heart, while witnessing an injustice.

Carla felt her face flush and guessed that her temperature was soaring to heights that no ordinary thermometer could ever hope to follow.

Suddenly Carla snatched up the package of miniature Christmas tree lights and headed for the cashier's counter as though it were her express ticket out of there. How good the fresh air would feel, cooling the temperature that raged within her body. As she slid the package across the counter, she noticed that the brawny merchant's complexion had pretty much returned to its normal color. "Well, well, who are you buying the lights for, Carla?" He sounded surprisingly good-natured and calm now.

The answer to his question seemed clearly self-evident, and Carla wondered if he wasn't trying to redeem his reputation as a good guy after the inhuman way he'd treated those men. More likely, it was just his idea of small talk. "It's for us, Mother and me." But when that didn't seem to entirely satisfy him, she felt called upon to add, "For our Christmas tree."

Her predictable answer appeared to stun the merchant. "Well, I'll be a monkey's uncle—your momma know what you're doing?"

Could there be something about Christmas lights that she didn't understand? she wondered. Could they be a little dangerous, maybe needing special handling, a little like fireworks? "Well, yes sir," she answered, feeling vaguely humiliated. She handed the merchant a neatly folded ten-dollar bill. "This is the money my mother gave me to buy Christmas tree decorations."

Mr. Harris cocked his large head to one side as though he were checking to make sure she was telling the truth. "You know something? That surprises me, sugar, it really does—espcially when you take into account all the whooping and hollering your mother did a couple of years back when Rachetville tried putting our own creche in front of our own city hall! And on our town's very own property at that! Well, behavior like that might be just the ticket with some of those free-loading, nuts-and-berries free spirits in Parson Springs, but that kind of stuff doesn't go in this town!"

Carla's head drooped against her chest the way the challenger's did when the champ had landed his killer punch against the poor guy's midsection in Saturday night's Television Fight of the Week. But unlike the luckless challenger, who remained flat-out on the canvas, her head rose slowly up, up, up again, almost level with Mr. Harris's eyes.

Sticking up for Judith had, over the years, become almost automatic. Never, never pleasureable, but still and all, automatic. "What my mother attempted to do," she explained slowly, giving each word a kind of resonating importance, "was to fight for the Constitution of the United States of America, and for what it says in there about the separation of church and state."

"You gotta be kidding! Think *our* Constitution needs help from *your* mother? Well, I don't! I fought for our country, risked my life over in Korea—so I ought to know!"

Carla stared into Mr. Harris's eyes just so he'd understand that he wasn't dealing with some little lightweight nothing that could oh-so-easily be tossed and thrown by the first gust of wind that came her way. "Well, in her own way, I believe Mother has fought for this country, too. She's fought for the right of everybody to choose their own beliefs even if they're different from your beliefs or mine."

Mr. Harris threw the change upon the counter. Carla, careful not to appear as though she were in flight, picked it up and with her head held high walked out of the store. Maybe the merchant understood now what he hadn't understood before. Nobody can get away with talking bad about her mom! Not even Andy Harris's daddy.

In a town where change is suspect, Rachetville's chief librarian, Carla's mother Judith Wayland, had come in for more than her share of suspicion. More

17

than anyone else, Carla wished that it just wasn't so. While publicly she would spring to her mother's defense at any provocation, privately—very privately—she was embarrassed and even angry that her mother couldn't pretty much share the same general opinions as everybody else. Or at the very least, why couldn't she keep opinions that were not ordinary everyday opinions to herself?

After all, if they were good enough for everybody else, why couldn't they be good enough for Judith? Her different thinking was not just a small matter, because being different caused problems. At last month's town meeting, Mrs. Hilda Wooten stood up and suggested: "Our public library could easily save some of the town's hard-earned money and be patriotic both at once—killing two birds with one stone, so to speak. The town library should make it a sworn policy not to buy any books, newspapers, or magazines that are critical of our country, our religion, or our American way."

The ringing applause for Mrs. Wooten hadn't entirely died down when Carla's mother was on her feet. First she quoted a poet from long ago comparing a public library to an evergreen tree because it went on blossoming all year long, but quoting that poet wasn't what got folks so upset. It was what she said next that caused all the trouble: ". . . as your town's chief librarian, I cannot in good conscience agree that we have too many books or periodicals that are critical of religion or government. The fact of the matter is that we have too few. If we lose our right to criticize, the next thing we'll lose is our right to be free. You see, in my opinion, it is the business of a library to help make the world *safe for diversity*."

Judith's remarks were followed by a silence so cold

and hard that it would have taken a chain saw to cut through it. A few people from the back of the room anonymously booed. When Hilda Wooten stood up to respond to Judith, she received an honest-to-goodness standing ovation! And that was even *before* she spoke what came to be much-quoted soul-stirring words: "It would be far better for both our community and for our country, Mrs. Wayland, if you'd forget about that diversity nonsense and instead use your God-given talents to help make the world *ripe for Christianity*."

Carla had grown up listening to her mother's sometimes funny and often depressing stories about how she barely survived the narrow mental and emotional confines of St. Joseph's Academy of Lafayette, Louisiana. More than once, the girl had been overcome with the need to protect her mother from the indignities of times past. If only she could, Carla would have willingly hurled herself backward through space and time to save her mother from nuns who struggled mightily to press Judith's free and far-ranging spirit into molds that bruised and bound.

Back in the middle 1960s when Judith would confide to her own mother the indignities that Sister Mary Staten, in particular, would subject the students to—particularly the dumber boys—her mother would only make those little *tsk tsk tsk*ing sounds. But when the girl wouldn't take heed of the *tsk*s to change the subject, then her distressed mother would begin pleading: "Stop it this minute! Stop talking badly about the nuns! Don't you know they can't do wrong because they're married to Jesus?"

Carla loved her mother, and in part because of so many long-ago anecdotes like these, she more than most daughters understood her mother. Understanding someone else's pain may not be all there is to love, but surely it's got to be a part of love.

Judith would stand up and speak out for things that others were against, and she was often absolutely opposed to what others favored. She was, for example, *for* sex education but opposed to Bible reading in the schools. She was *for* a woman's right to an abortion, but she was *against* the way the largest local employer, Tyson Chicken, discarded poultry entrails.

All you had to do was open your ears and listen when Judith Wayland's name popped up, and you'd see that suddenly there'd be an awful lot of *yeah but*s injected into the conversation. Carla admired her mother for her courage and yet she sometimes longed for a different kind of a mother, one that wasn't controversial at all.

Chapter 4

A CHEER AS mighty as it was spontaneous bounced throughout Rachetville High at three-fifteen in the afternoon that began the nine days of Christmas holidays! As Carla and Debby Packard, her best friend ever since they shared a playpen together, headed quickly for the west door, Carla heard her name ricocheting against the plaster walls.

Andy Harris was galloping up to them. "Hey, Carla, hey, where you running off to?"

"Oh, Andy, hi," she said, thrilled and surprised that he was at long last seeking her out. At the same time she was disappointed in herself that after wishing and waiting for months for this wondrous event to happen, the best she could come up with was "Hi, Andy." Wouldn't she have given her entire kingdom for some perky little sophisticated zinger of a response?

She was interested in Andy not merely because he

was cute and good-looking—although, the good Lord knows, he sure *was* cute and good-looking! It was all really a little strange, especially to Carla, exactly the way her feelings for Andy ignited.

One bright Sunday morning in late summer, Carla caught sight of the Harris family, Bibles in hand, hurrying across Grove Street. Mr. and Mrs. Harris, along with their two grammar school daughters and Andy, were on their way to services at the Rachetville Baptist Church.

Their clothes were stylish enough to command attention and maybe even respect anywhere—New York, Boston—anywhere! Mr. Harris especially looked successful enough to have his picture plastered across the jacket of one of those How-to-Make-a-Million-Bucks-in-Your-Spare-Time books.

Although Carla still felt annoyed with Mr. Harris's inexcusable actions toward the men in the store, as well as his digs against her mother, she was (in spite of herself) deeply drawn to this seemingly all-American, perfect-looking family. She had done what she had to do—stick up for her mother—but her admiration for the merchant existed in a way she couldn't deny.

For one thing, he was totally unlike Roy Wayland, the father that she had never met. Mr. Harris stuck with his family, working hard and providing well for them. And what a relief it must be when your beliefs seem to custom fit those of the community. Maybe most appealing of all to Carla was the fact that the Harris family so beautifully blended into this town. Never would a person connected by blood or marriage to the Harrises ever know what it was to feel like an outcast!

Then there was Mrs. Harris. Elna Harris was so sweet and pretty and nice that she just wouldn't know how to upset anybody. Probably not even if she tried because she was a true-blue Southern lady—taught to flatter and charm men, never to challenge them. Which was fine with Elna because all her ideas had already been handed down to her from everybody else.

The Harris children included two kid sisters and Andy—handsome Andy with chin high and carrying his very own leather-bound Bible. Although he was still young, a person could just tell that he was someday going to make a name, a very big name, for himself!

That's when Carla was overwhelmed with the sense that she didn't want to be publicly connected with her controversial mother. She needed to belong to a handsome and respectable family. And she needed it *now*!

At the precise moment of that realization, she grasped what all her old, unnamed, and as yet unfaced yearnings were all about. But at the next moment, when she thought of her own mother's cheerful sacrifices on her behalf, she felt distinctly disloyal. She knew she should feel ashamed of herself—and she did feel smudged with shame because nobody, absolutely nobody, could have done more, would have done more to raise a daughter alone than Judith Wayland.

When a lot of parents were collapsing mindlessly in front of the tube, Judith would be happily swapping stories about her day or reviewing Carla's homework assignments. And who but her mother would have early-on hooked her on to the greater and grander world beyond Rachetville, Arkansas, through books? One of Carla's earliest memories of her mom was of her whispering into her ear, "Inside every good book is a secret." But it wasn't until Carla was an awful lot older that she came to understand that those "secrets" her mother had dangled before her questing eyes had more to do with the pains, the sorrows, and the joys of being human than they ever did with secret hiding places or buried treasure.

Carla came to believe that there was a direct correlation between her being "very understanding" and the books that she had read. All her friends commented on her quality of being good at listening. So for her the *real* value of books was not merely to increase her vocabulary or to give her a wealth of fascinating facts, but to allow her to have emotional experiences far beyond her own limited existence.

Without Judith's influence, her own sharply felt appreciation of others and what they felt would probably have been more blunt. Carla knew that she had so very much to be grateful for, and she *did* feel grateful, yet sometimes she felt angry, too! Angry that she had to stand up and take the backlash as well as the occasional tongue-lash for her controversial mother. Why couldn't she just be a member of a totally respected, completely uncontroversial family, a family like the Harrises?

There was anger, too, that Judith's choice of a husband had been such a poor one, leaving Judith husbandless and Carla fatherless. That made Carla determined that when the time came for her to marry, things would be different. As she watched that handsome and prosperous Harris family cross Grove Street, she thought how wonderful it would be if she could be disowned by Judith and adopted by Larry and Elna. And the second thought she had was how terribly shabby her first thought was. She stopped right there on Grove Street and asked herself how could she even think of such a thing. But as a matter of fact, she *did* think of such a thing—and, what was worse, she thought about it a lot.

"Hey, you know, I was just thinking about you," Andy Harris was saying. He flashed first Carla and then Debby a smile so dazzling that it looked as though he were auditioning for a toothpaste ad. "I was wondering if you've recuperated yet?"

"Recuperated?" *Damn!* Why didn't she know what he was talking about? Her mind had really wandered. "Uh . . . from what?"

"You were in our store yesterday—I saw you—don't tell me you missed that really gross stuff that went on!"

"Carla, I'm really sorry, but I've got to go," Debby broke in. "I promised some of the kids that I'd meet them at Lindy's house and I'm already late."

"I'll call you tonight," Carla yelled at the back of her already departing friend. She thought how Debby Packard had given her one more reason to love her. Knowing when you're not wanted and knowing exactly when and how to make a graceful departure, well, Debby couldn't have done it better if they had been rehearsing it for years.

Andy scrunched his thick, though naturally well-shaped, eyebrows together in a way that made it clear that he was about to say something serious. "Some people . . ." He began shaking his head just as though he were wishing it weren't so. "The way some people act . . ." He whistled low through his front teeth. "It's enough to make me puke, honest to God!"

Carla was more than relieved, she was downright thrilled to learn that Andy was as outraged by the two strangers' public humiliation as she was. The previous night, when she had told Judith about the confrontations, first between the men and the lady, then between the men and the merchant, one of the first questions her mother asked was, "And what was Andy's reaction to the emotional bloodbath?"

"He didn't like it one bit more than I did!" she replied proudly. Even though she hadn't actually seen Andy respond one way or the other, she was certain that someone as special as Andrew Anthony Harris would find it every bit as terrible as she had. And, thank goodness, he had, because—well, he was just that kind of a person!

"Boy, do I ever know what you mean, Andy," she told him. "I can't understand . . . I mean I guess I just don't understand why people who call themselves grown up would behave that way!" Carla wondered if maybe she wasn't speaking a little too frankly, since one of the people being criticized was, after all, his very own father.

"Know what I think should be done?" he asked her, managing to sound both masculine and decisive. "I can tell you how to put an end to that kind of stuff real quick!"

"You can?" Carla thought he must be really smart, 'cause for as long as people have been on this earth, they'd wondered how and why and when some people just seem to come into this world hating. She was pleased that he had not only thought long and hard about this problem, but was now about to describe his actual workable solutions. "Really?"

"The answer is already there in the Bible! In Romans, where it as plain as day says: 'The wages of sin are death.' If I were president, first thing I'd do is to make death for homosexuality the law. But I wouldn't do it just like that!" he said, snapping his fingers. "I'd give everybody maybe ten days of fair notice, you know, like a grace period. But after that, well, all fags who won't stop being fags, well, I'd give them the mandatory death sentence. Treat queers the same way we treat murderers, let them all fry to a frizzle in the electric chair."

"You'd fry them in the electric chair?" she repeated, making certain through her shock and disappointment that she had heard correctly. She thought of her friend with the red scarf who had whispered words of kindness to her. Wasn't it time—way past time—to defend him? "You can't do that! You can't electrocute someone for *being* something. You can only electrocute people for *doing* something."

Andy exploded. "But they do *do* something! Don't you *know* anything, girl? They commit the sin of sodomy, and that's as bad as you can get. You know, you don't have to believe me, you can read all about it in the Bible. The Bible calls it an abomination—an *a-bom-in-a-tion*." He emphatically separated and then sounded out each syllable, just in case she didn't understand the word the first time around.

It was all very confusing. Carla wondered if maybe she was a bad person because she didn't hate homosexuals the way good and pious Christians were supposed to. Loving someone of the same sex seemed to be okay if it wasn't sexual, like the way she felt about her mother. And, of course, she loved her best friend Debby Packard since they were toddlers.

"Hey, you know you don't have to believe me!" Andy's words came crashing through her thoughts, scattering them to the distant recesses of her brain. And yet this much she did know: She was not concerned about being drawn to someone of her own sex because she was far more sexually drawn to someone of the opposite sex.

Andy socked his fist into his open palm. "It says in Leviticus that if a man lies with a man that's an abomination and both men will be put to death!"

Carla tried without success to picture God torturing the man with the red scarf to death, but her imagination didn't seem to want to stretch that far. "That just doesn't sound right. I don't think a compassionate God (and the Bible does speak of him as being compassionate) would punish anyone for what they can't help. I don't believe that God is like that!"

"Can't help it?!" Andy's voice was shrill with righteous indignation. "That's about the dumbest thing I've ever heard—are you kidding me or what? To stop being queers all they have to do is stop doing what they do— or don't you know that?"

The girl felt torn between being agreeably likable or being disagreeable—more true to her convictions—and not so likable. She decided to race for the middle ground, for the more intellectual and less emotional middle ground. "I read somewhere how scientists are finding chemical differences in the bodies of homosexuals. So if they prove that—that God with his own hands made these people the way they are—then why on earth would he punish them for being different?"

Andy was shaking his head so vigorously that for a moment Carla worried that it might possibly come flying off his neck. After finally gaining Andy's interest, was she being stupid to toss it all away over a simple matter of opinion? "You can't believe anything you read in the media," he interjected at her first pause. "Satan, led by non-Christians and other atheists, run that show. The Bible says, 'The bread of deceit is sweet to a man; but afterwards, his mouth is filled with gravel.' You know. . ." He paused before concluding, "It's just as simple as that!"

"Sounds like you really know an awful lot about the Bible. Did you learn all of that at church?" she asked. Carla decided that there seemed to be plenty of holes in his logic but she wasn't eager to comment on that just yet.

Andy smiled and Carla breathed easier. She hadn't wanted to lose him even before she'd gotten him to be hers. "Well, we've got cable so I watch a lot of the preachers, especially Jerry Falwell and Jimmy Swaggart. They're my favorites. And we've got a real good preacher now at the Rachetville Baptist, Reverend Roland Wheelwright. So I pretty much stay awake and listen. Say, speaking of staying awake, you oughta see my old man."

"Really?"

"Oh, yeah. It might be all in his mind or else something psychological, but as soon as he walks in the door of our church he begins to yawn, and when he sits down in one of those pews—*watch out!*"

"You don't mean it—he falls asleep?"

"Worse than that! He snores like a chain saw—or he would if my mother would let him. Only he doesn't 'cause she'd put a hole in his ribs with her sharp little ol' elbow, honest to God she would!"

Carla laughed delightedly. She always thought that anyone with the pert, wide-eyed look of Andy Harris would almost have to have a sense of humor, but she never really knew for sure, at least not until this moment. That pleased her almost as much as the fact that he didn't do the expected thing and say good-bye as soon as they reached the corner of Main and Union.

Instead, he turned down Union with her and started walking her home, while talking about how important his mother was to his finding Christ. "I guess she saw that no matter how hard she tried she couldn't for the life of her get Dad saved, so she sort of doubled up her efforts on getting me born again."

"Just the same, it must do your father's heart good to see that you're such a good Christian," suggested Carla.

"You don't know my dad!" the boy shot back. "That

man has practically no respect for little 'limp-wristed, tea-sipping parasites.' That's what he calls ministers and all *truly* committed Christian men: 'limp-wristed, tea-sipping parasites.' Now can you imagine that?"

"That's surprising. I've seen your entire family on Sunday morning hurrying across Grove Street on their way to the Rachetville Baptist."

"Oh, more often than not," Andy agreed pleasantly. "He gets pulled along on a Sunday morning. But according to him, it's okay, even respectable for a man to go, only it's not okay to treat church really seriously. Know what he tells me? He says, 'Peabrain'—I love that little joke of his, calling me 'Peabrain.' He says, 'Peabrain, marry yourself a good woman and forget all this religious stuff, 'cause she'll do praying enough for you both!'"

"He calls you 'Peabrain'?" Carla protested. "That's so cruel, and not one bit fair because anyone can tell that you're ... I mean ... you're really intelligent. I hope you don't let him get away with that!"

"He thinks *he's* so smart!" Andy paused to silently savor her compliment. "Because, you see, nobody gave him anything, but just the same he's single-handedly built up a really big business. What with the store and his mail-order business, he's doing a whole lot better than okay. I can guarantee you that!"

Carla couldn't remember ever having heard anybody complain and brag about a person in practically the same sentence. "That doesn't for a minute give him the right to put you down!" Her voice rang with conviction.

"Well," he said slowly, as though waiting to be convinced, "one of these days ... one of these days I'm going to strike back. And won't he be surprised?"

Without much success, she searched his face for the

resolve that she couldn't exactly locate anywhere among his words. She came right out and asked, "What do you intend to do?"

For several moments he was quiet, as though he now had to think about something that he had never gotten around to thinking about before. "Well, I've been thinking about buying a set of barbells, you know, build up my pectorals. So the next time he wants to arm wrestle, *wham,* I'll have him pinned on the table before he knows what hit him!" Andy's face lit up with pleasure-to-be. "And another thing I'll do is the next time he gets mad at me, telling me that I couldn't compete with an orangutan and then ending with one of his favorite brags: 'I won the rat race . . .' I'm going to answer him back."

"How?" asked Carla, her brains buzzing in search of Andy's perfect comeback.

"Well, I think maybe I'll . . ."

"What?" Carla blurted out, anticipating Andy's thoughtfully engineered response.

"Hmm, well, I'm not sure . . . I'm still working on it."

"I've got it!" she cried. "Look him straight in the eye and tell him that anyone who wins the rat race is still a rat!"

Andy grinned broadly, clapping his hands together. "*Wow!* That's good! That's real good!"

Carla returned his smile happily. She had just figured out the first thing she would write in her diary tonight: "Today is a day that I'll never forget because I waited so long for it to happen. Today is the day that Andy Harris walked me home."

Chapter 5

ON CHRISTMAS MORNING something happened in Parson Springs, the next town over, that had not happened there on Christmas day for twenty-seven years. It snowed. And this time it wasn't so sparse that defiant blades of grass kept poking on through the thin, white covering all over the place. This was an inch or more of the real stuff, enough and plenty to wrap the town up like a magical Christmas present in a sparkling cover of dazzling white.

In the predawn hours, as the young and not-so-young woke to check under the Christmas tree, living-room lights were switched on all over this Ozark Mountain community. The village of Parson Springs was built up and down and around the side of Magic Mountain like a corkscrew. If viewed from high and far enough away, it looked like a giant Christmas tree floating in space, each gaily lit house dangling from a branch like a carefully chosen ornament.

A festive Christmas tree stood in the corner of Frank and Stephan's frame house. Pieces of wrapping paper and broken ribbons were strewn everywhere as impatient Stephan walked briskly into the room. Ignoring the big cuckoo clock that bonged and the round clock that noiselessly told the time, he glanced nervously at his wristwatch before yelling up the stairs, "All right, Frank, this is it! If you can't get yourself together in time for church, you can jolly well stay home. I'm leaving now because enough is enough is enough! You hear me? I'm not kidding! I mean it!"

Frank strolled leisurely into the living room, brushing some imaginary lint from the sleeve of his well-tailored pin-striped suit. "Hear ye, hear ye, all you women and girls of Atkins County, Arkansas," he chanted. "Be prepared on this bright Christmas morning to eat your heart out because neither Mr. Jones nor Mr. Montgomery is available."

For six years prior to coming to Parson Springs last May, Stephan Jones and Frank Montgomery had been co-owners of a tiny antique shop on Boston's famous Beacon Hill. Every year their profits increased by a reassuring fifteen to twenty percent, and they thought they could go on forever. If it hadn't been for the new lease their landlord sent demanding double the rent, they probably would have, too.

Since they had no choice but to move, they decided to change things completely. They decided to move to a place where the rent would be cheap, the climate would be agreeable, and the people, long known for their Southern hospitality, would be friendly.

Although Frank was born, raised, educated, and

finally even employed in Boston, he had in recent years begun to itch to experience life in another corner of the country. For Stephan, who had come to the city when he was eighteen burning with the desire to become a Jesuit priest and lead men to Christ, Boston would always be the scene of his failure. For the thirty months that he had studied at the Weston School of Theology, he had tried to work from inside the church to help Catholics teach a kinder, more open, and less fearful vision of the homosexual.

But little by little, the closet homosexual with his equally closeted agenda began to grow steadily more and more discouraged. So much that he woke on the morning of his twenty-first birthday with the stark realization that if he wanted to hold onto his faith, he had to leave divinity school. And he had to leave it at once!

More than eight years after that decision, Stephan and his partner spent weeks discussing, arguing, and researching the painful but still exciting prospect of finding another more suitable home for themselves and their antique business. Finally all cities and towns were eliminated from consideration except one: Parson Springs, the artsy-craftsy town on Arkansas's famed tourist trail.

Stephan sighed as he remembered the first person they met on arrival—Billy Saul Baxter, the town's only real estate man. He had stuck a pudgy finger toward the crest of the mountain where a seven-hundred foot high concrete Jesus was visible for miles in any direction. "Our mountain town is known far and wide as the crown jewel," Billy Saul enthused. "On the glittering buckle known as the Bible Belt!"

On this Christmas morning Stephan drove the only vehicle they owned—an oversized RV down the highway toward the next town of Ratchetville. He was gambling that the live wire of a preacher over at the First Baptist Church of Ratchetville would hold Frank's interest better than the monotone priest had over at Our Lady of the Mountain Chapel. For Stephan, denomination was nothing, what meant everything was seeing his life partner accept Jesus as his Lord and Savior.

Stephan prepared to turn their RV into the parking lot of the Rachetville Baptist Church. "Oh, no! Would you look at that, Frank. There's not a space anywhere! See, didn't I tell you? Would it have hurt if we'd have left fifteen minutes earlier?"

"Keep on heading down Main Street, Stevie, there's another church at the end of the block, surrounded by a parking lot."

"But I don't want any other church," Stephan objected, guiding the motorized behemoth onto a yellow-striped section of asphalt where a standing sign solemnly announced: THOU SHALT NOT PARK. "It's not as though we don't have a Baptist church in Parson Springs," Frank remarked. "Why did we have to come over here?"

Pointing dramatically at the majestic spire of the imposing red-brick, Colonial-style church, Stephan answered, "Well, open your eyes and look at it! Just look at it, would you? Can't you just tell that here at last is a church that will embrace us?"

Frank gazed up at the bell tower, squinting against the morning sun. "No, I can't honestly say that I can."

Stephan's eyes scanned the church. He shrugged. "You don't suppose it reminds me of the Baptist church that I used to attend with the Protestant side of my family back in Arlington, Massachusetts? Those were good old days."

They hurried up the granite steps, passing without taking much notice of the glass window whose purpose was to advertise to all those on the outside what went on inside.

THE RACHETVILLE BAPTIST CHURCH
Welcomes You to Fellowship in Christ
Reverend Roland B. Wheelwright
Special Christmas Sermon:
"What Did You Give Jesus on His Day?"
After church social—refreshments
Rec Room

As the newcomers entered, people nodded and smiled. One woman who looked as though she might have come into this world past middle age called out, "Welcome, strangers! Smile and be happy, you hear, 'cause you're with God's people now." All this friendly and benign attention by all these well-scrubbed and sweet-sounding people was so pleasant, it didn't take Frank and Stephan long to begin to feel as though maybe they really did belong after all.

At a pew toward the center rear of the church sat Carla, thrilled at actually having maneuvered her mother into a place of worship. Anyone seeing Judith for the first time would likely be surprised. She had lustrous auburn hair, eyes that glowed with compassion, and a delicate facial structure, but then so did her daughter. What was most surprising was that the larger-than-life librarian was really small of stature.

During the singing of the opening hymn, "O Little Town of Bethlehem," Carla whispered to her mother, "Well, Mom, isn't it nice? Aren't you glad I made you come?"

"It *is* architecturally appealing," admitted Judith. "And the music's surprisingly good. Nice choir."

"Oh, do you think we could become members?" the girl asked.

Although Judith realized that she had been manipulated into coming to Andy's church, she was good-natured about it. "Oh, come on now, Carla, asking me to join a congregation just because you fancy one of its members is not really the soundest of reasons. At any rate, could we at least table this discussion until *after* Reverend Wheelwright's sermon?"

When the last note of the hymn was sung a hush that said something important was coming fell over the worshipers. Then the Reverend Roland B. Wheelwright, a handsome man with a full head of white hair, strode purposefully toward the raised pulpit. He wore a dramatic black robe with vibrant maroon trim that had been custom-made by a Jewish designer of liturgical wear on New York City's Seventh Avenue. Before uttering a single word, he paused as though to heighten the dramatic effect while allowing an expression of supreme beatitude to play across his manly features. Finally, he intoned, "Brothers and sisters in Christ, my sermon for this Christmas morning is: 'What did you give Our Savior on his birthday?' "

The preacher started his sermon like a mild-mannered holy man, but he didn't stay mild for very long. "The Bible teaches us to plant the seed, to sow the seed. You want to prosper? Then you give to the Lord's church! Give all you can! Give until it hurts and then give some more! Do that and watch how Jesus will return your gift a hundredfold—nay, a thousandfold!"

"Inspiring," Frank whispered, amid a yawn. "Truly inspiring."

With his elbow, Stephan gave him a behave-yourself nudge and Frank struggled to keep his eyes open.

"We Christian soldiers have got to offer up our lives to fight on the front line with Jesus' army! Because, and make no mistake about it . . ." His voice calmed down and became lower and almost intimate. "Oh, my dear, dear brothers and sisters in Christ, how can I warn you? How can I let you know?" Now his voice began to rise. "Satan is all the time getting bolder!"

His face flushed red, and Frank thought it looked close to the color of the center of a medium-rare filet mignon. Staring transfixed at the ornate church ceiling above, the minister banged his bare fist on the ornate hand-carved pulpit, then clasped both hands together. "Oh, Lord Jesus, teach us that we can do a hundred good deeds, and still not enter the kingdom of heaven. Or a hundred thousand good deeds and it will be as nothing in your eyes if we are not washed in your sanctifying blood. In the blood of Our Savior, Jesus Christ. Glory! Glory! Thank you Jesus! Thank you Jesus!" He swabbed his sweating face with an oversized handkerchief, but he continued without pause. "Oh, God, wash us sinners in the cleansing blood of Jesus Christ who died for our sins on Calvary. And then send us out in glory to join your army. Jesus' army! Hallelujah! Hallelujah!

"Wearing the cross of Jesus, we will be fighters against Satan, and it matters not in which guise he appears. Take warning all you pornographers!" he shouted, lunging with an imaginary sword against an imaginary enemy. "Take warning all you child molesters!" He lunged a second time. "Take warning all you homosexuals!" And this time his lunge was the most violent lunge of all. "We Christian soldiers are going to smite you! Are you listening to me, Satan?! I'm telling you! I'm warning you! 'Cause we're going to up and *smite you dead*!"

"What do you suppose ever happened to the Prince

of Peace?" Judith whispered with obvious disdain to her daughter. Carla was so preoccupied with staring at the back of Andy Harris's well-proportioned head and daydreaming that she hardly paid enough attention to the preaching to comment.

Six rows behind them, Frank spoke directly into Stephan's ear. "What you said a while back about this church *embracing* us. Didn't you get your verbs mixed up, old buddy? Didn't you mean to say *impaling* us?"

At the conclusion of the services, Mrs. Wheelwright, a big woman with a seemingly baked-on smile, stood just inside the front door with her husband exchanging Christmas greetings with the departing parishioners. Since new faces are the most obvious sign that a church is growing in strength and prestige, the minister enthusiastically pumped Frank's and Stephan's hands before inquiring if they weren't newcomers to Rachetville.

The men explained that they were former Bostonians who lived in the next town over, in Parson Springs, where they had opened the Forgotten Treasures Antique Shop. Mr. Wheelwright smiled even more broadly as he muttered something about "businessmen being the backbone of any community. Yes sir, they're the very backbone of this country!" He became, if possible, even more enthusiastic than before.

"We're honored that you fine Christian gentlemen saw fit to pray with us today." He chuckled a little— a little this-is-just-between-us-guys chuckle—before continuing. "Now I know you must know that there's a fine, gospel-preaching Baptist church right in your own community?" The minister paused expectantly, clearly trying to extract a much-hoped-for compliment, which Stephan politely supplied. "Well, yes of course, we did know about the Johnson Memorial Baptist Church, and I've been there to services, too, but frankly I guess we were seeking something different. Something more dynamic."

Reverend Wheelwright accepted what he *thought* was a compliment amid his ongoing nods and broad smiles. "Well, glad you could make it, really am—well, now, let me introduce you fellows to another one of our fine Rachetville businessmen and his lovely family. Larry! Larry and Elna Jean Harris!" the preacher shouted, and then vigorously beckoned to them amid the exiting throng. "You and your handsome family march yourselves right on over here!" When Elna heard their minister ringing out their names, her face lit up with an unspoken but unmistakable pride.

By the time the entire Harris family had snaked their way through the crowd to reach Reverend Wheelwright's side, he already had one arm around Frank and the other around Stephan. It took Larry and Andy a glance, and then a second much longer stare, before it struck them, even before the preacher had concluded his introduction, exactly who those men in the warm embrace of their glowingly happy pastor were.

Larry and Andy could not have looked more stricken if they had been struck across the face with a two-by-four, but Elna wasn't suffering along with them; she seemed supremely happy. Elna was blissfully unaware that the two men she was now smiling and fluttering her heavily mascared lashes at were the same "two queers" that her husband had come home ranting and raving about a few days before. She wasn't even bothering to hide the fact that she was obviously much affected by the strangers, but in a way precisely the opposite from what her husband and son would have wished.

Stephan and Frank recognized the male members of the Harris family but managed to keep wearing their faintest of smiles while Elna acted as though she were giving flirting lessons. "Well, I do declare," she confided to them. "Why, I'm going to tell you right now that we Southern women are going to be quicker and smarter than those foolish Yankee women that let you two precious fellows get away! Not even if I live to be a hundred will I ever understand how they'd let a terrible thing like that happen."

"Mother!" said Andy, squeezing her forearm.

"Elna Jean!" spoke Larry in words that sounded as though they had been pulled screaming through clenched teeth.

"Now what has gotten into you two?" Mrs. Harris lyrically asked while quickly glancing sideways at both her son and her husband. "You just hold your horses, honey, 'cause I'm not fixing to leave this spot until I show these handsome Yankees a little of our good ol' Southern hospitality." She turned her full and admiring gaze back to the strangers. "Now I just happen to know two of the sweetest girls that God ever blew breath into—from good Christian homes too—who'd jump at the chance to meet such precious fellows as you all."

Frank's eyes caught and then held Elna's eyes, and surprisingly that seemed to noticeably wind down her chatter, at least long enough for him to speak. "Stephan and I appreciate your kind offer, we really do, but we must decline. Now if you'll excuse us, Mrs. Harris, we really must be going."

Outside Judith and Carla were walking together toward the church's parking lot as Carla was attempting to infuse her mother with her own enthusiasm for the largest and most talked-about church in town. "Oh, I loved it, Mother, I really did—the flowers, the music, everything! And did you see everybody who was there? Just like the Who's Who of Atkins County."

"I'm pleasantly surprised to learn that you saw anybody *besides* Andy Harris," said Judith as she stopped at the driver's side of her aged Volvo to reach deep into her purse for ignition keys.

"Fooled you, didn't I?" Carla laughed. "I saw Mayor Edwards with his new wife, Coach Early, Ginny and Paul Williams, Tom and Jeannette Hackett. . . ."

"I wonder why it is," Judith asked as crinkles formed over her high, cool forehead, "that if you pushed organized religion on your kids, they'd reject it, but don't give it to them and they scream for it. Somebody please tell me why?"

The same crinkle that was on Judith's forehead now was on Carla's. "Oh, I don't know, Mom, only don't make it complicated because it's not! I just think that it's time that we stopped being outsiders and joined something bigger than ourselves. This church, you'll have to admit, is the absolute perfect church to join and Reverend Wheelwright is a real dynamo. Andy thinks he's great. Don't you agree?"

Judith took a right turn on Main Street, passed the town square with its garish string of alternating red and green Christmas lights, and thought once again how very dreary downtown Rachetville really was. The Atkins County Courthouse was the only nineteenth-century building in town that actually survived into the twentieth century. It was also, arguably, Rachetville's most preserved and beautiful edifice, and the fact that the courthouse sat on a square patch of lime-green grass added to its grandeur.

Even though she was wearing her sunglasses, Judith

squinted in the unaccustomed brightness of sun and snow. "Reverend Wheelwright? Believe me, you don't want to know," she said after a pause, "what I think."

"I honestly don't think you could help giving me your opinion, Mom, 'cause admit it—you've got more opinions than anyone I know. Why even your opinions have opinions!"

At that, Judith reacted. "All right, you asked for it, and you're going to get it! You want to know what I think? I think he's a living, breathing bigot who believes, or pretends to believe, that Jesus Christ whispers only in his ears. And therefore he, and only he, as Christ's messenger, is qualified to lead all of us pathetic sinners to salvation."

"Oh, Mother, why do you *always* do that?"

"Always do *what*?"

"See things that nobody else sees?" Carla's voice was pitched a good half an octave higher than usual. "I never heard Reverend Wheelwright say that Jesus whispers in his ear, not once!"

"Then allow me to back up so that I may be as accurate as I know how." If Carla in her excitement had pitched her voice higher than usual, then Judith's pitch seemed consciously and noticeably lower than usual. "What the good pastor said was that Jesus had spoken to him 'in his spirit,' telling how deeply disturbed he was by the continuing gay rights activists picketing in front of the Arkansas statehouse. So what does Jesus do? Jesus of Nazareth, Son of the Living God, bypasses the five billion people now inhabiting this globe to speak directly (via, no doubt, some great celestial eight-hundred number in the sky) to none other than our very own Reverend Roland Wheelwright. Explaining to the Reverend Wheelwright precisely what he should tell his congregation today. And so presumably he did."

"So . . . what's wrong with that? That's just the way preachers talk. Everybody *knows* that's just the way they talk, only nobody else treats it all that seriously. At least nobody but you!"

Without any comment other than the tightening of her hands on the steering wheel, the librarian made a left turn into the third driveway on River Street, and in front of the freshly painted single-car garage, she cut her motor and then turned to face her daughter. "Let's just say that I have *real* trouble believing that the only way I can get through to God is through his only son, Jesus of Nazareth, and the only way I can get on line with the son is by first going through his only earthly spokesman, Roland Wheelwright."

The girl shook her head with clear disgust. "Oh, please . . . you're making the Baptists out to be a lot worse than they are! He can be a spokesman for Jesus without his being Jesus' *only* spokesman. Now can't you at least admit to that?"

Judith jerked the keys from the ignition. "And did you happen to notice that the good reverend has an assistant minister named Weldner? Does that mean that you have to first go through Reverend Weldner to reach Reverend Wheelwright who will put you through to Jesus Christ who in turn will put you through to God?"

"I can't talk to you when you're like this!" said Carla, who jumped out of the car and began walking double time toward the front door.

"Hey!" said Judith, racing up the front-door steps to touch her daughter's shoulder. "I'm sorry. Really I am! I should be able to state my honest concerns without stooping to ridicule."

"Then why do you do it, Mom, *why*?" Carla queried. "I know you believe in God because we've talked about it often enough! Is this ridicule only because one single nun, Sister Staten, was bad to you thirty years ago? Is that what this is all about?"

"I wish I could deny it, but I can't. That experience certainly started my distaste for organized religion—it started my questioning the entire process. And the nuns, not just Sister Staten but *all* the nuns, insisted that we were not to reason, but we were to accept the Church and its teachings *on faith*. That's what I was *always* taught, but it never came close to silencing the rumblings within me, the rumblings that kept asking, If God gave us the power of reason, then why would he ever want us to suspend that reason? Fish can swim better. Deer can run faster. Cats are quieter. Canaries can sing better.

"So if God gave me this one special gift, this ability to reason things out for myself, why, in God's name, would he ever want me to suspend that reason? I went to the nuns so they could help me sew up this gaping hole in my garment of faith. But their all-too-predictable response—'That's only the devil talking to you, child'—never even came close to covering my spiritual nakedness."

Judith searched her daughter's eyes as though asking—no, begging—for understanding. "I can tell you that for the first few years at St. Joseph's Academy—roughly from the time I was five to when I was nine or ten—I really believed that I must have been the most evil girl in the entire school. Because you see, I simply did not love the holy sisters the way I was supposed to."

Once inside the cheerful but old-style kitchen, the women went about their respective jobs without any unnecessary discussion. For a long time, all kitchen work had been divided roughly into two distinct categories: the creative and the noncreative. Under the creative came planning menus and making shopping lists, as well as doing the actual cooking, which was Carla's work. She took pride in doing it because she knew she did it well. Judith never interfered and never complained, not even when an occasional disaster struck and the results were less than wonderful.

For her part, Judith always much preferred the noncreative kitchen work that she could do almost completely by rote, allowing her mind to roam free and far. Her ideal jobs, for example, were scrubbing pots and setting the table.

By the time the paprika chicken, vegetable casserole, and noodles were taken piping hot from the oven and placed on the table next to the sunny breakfast-room window, it was almost one o'clock. Both women realized that they had come about as close as they could get to having a blowup without actually having one. Arguing was a downer at any time, but on Christmas day, for both mother and daughter, it would have been almost too upsetting to contemplate.

After the main course, but before the dessert, Carla touched the napkin to her mouth before asking, "Now that you understand that your anger toward Reverend Wheelwright is merely something neurotic left over from your parochial school days, do you think we could calmly and sensibly talk about joining his church?"

Judith lifted her eyebrows. "I never said that."

"Are you kidding? I *heard* you say it."

"Whatever you heard, you can be certain of this: You didn't hear me say that I have *no* objection to Mr. Wheelwright. It is not only perfectly possible, but it is perfectly true that one could have a bad parochial school experience and still be capable of making sound, rational judgments."

"What are you getting so testy about, Mom? I honestly don't see anything worth getting riled up about. Only thing I can see is you . . . you getting so damned worked up over . . . over nothing. Nothing!"

Suddenly Judith's eyes flashed fire and Carla could tell that she was about to receive far more of an answer than she had bargained for, far more of an answer than she had ever wanted. But then, just as Carla had emotionally buttoned herself down in preparation for the verbal assault that was a-coming, she heard her mother sigh deeply, and she knew that much of the anger had dissipated and was riding out on that sigh.

"You're quite right, of course," Judith admitted, "I am worked up. Things bother me that don't seem to bother anybody else. Injustice, for example, bothers me more than I can say. And when I see a man of God standing before the altar putting homosexuals in the same category as child molesters and pornographers— well, then, I'm more than bothered. I'm angry! I'm very, very angry because a minister of God has changed before my very eyes into a peddler of hate."

Carla shook her head no. "And there you go again, Mom! If Reverend Wheelwright was that . . . that peddler of hate like you say he is, then how come only *you* saw that? Explain that to me, 'cause I'd really, *really* be interested in knowing."

Judith shrugged. "Maybe I'm not the only one who saw it. Who knows? Maybe others saw it, too. Maybe everyone saw it. Maybe nobody saw it. But remember: An artichoke is still an artichoke regardless of how many or how few people can identify it. And hate is still hate, Carla, regardless of how many *or* how few recognize it."

"Just stop it!" Carla jumped up from the table. "He *is* a minister of God and whether you believe it or not, ministers of God are in the business of preaching love. Love! And another thing: Everybody respects and likes him, but with you it's different! Are you maybe a little upset because everybody respects you, but not everybody likes you? Well, I've got news for you. I'm tired of you finding fault with everything normal. I don't want to be like you, Mother. I want everybody to like me! So what if once in a while I have to pretend to like people I don't like or pretend to dislike people that I really like. What's the big deal? It's just that simple: I want to be liked. Why in all of your years of living haven't you found out what I've already learned: There's nothing more important or better than being liked!"

"You don't want to be like me. . . ." Judith repeated softly, looking at her daughter through eyes that were beginning to be touched by a light mist. "That's funny, so funny. . . ." A series of low, sad chuckles seemed to originate from somewhere deep within her.

Carla looked stricken as she followed her mother from the breakfast room into the book-lined living room with its small tree aglow with miniature lights. "What's so funny?" But when she received nothing in the way of a reply except a slow, solemn shaking of her mother's head, she demanded, "Mother, answer me, dammit!"

"How do I begin?" asked Judith as she took a seat in the only straight-backed chair in the room. Carla was not entirely certain whether Judith was gazing upward to seek heavenly inspiration or just because she was so fond of the vibrant foliage on her ceiling wallpaper—which, she said, reminded her of a place she had always hoped to see, but never had: a tropical rain forest.

Carla sat quietly but uneasily across from her before finally asking, "Will you please tell me what you're thinking?"

Judith sighed audibly and then her gaze dropped from tropical forests to her daughter's eyes. "I think you should know that I wasn't exactly born Judith Wayland who could always be counted on to come out punching for what she believed was right. Actually, when you were a baby, I'm afraid that I more resembled a frightened mouse than a lion for truth and justice."

"*You* a frightened mouse! You've got to be kidding."

Judith's head rose up and then slowly fell back down again. "The thing is, I was so desperate to please Roy so that you would have a father and I would have a husband that I was terrified of possessing a single opinion that wasn't precisely *his* opinion. And that, incidentally, is not offered as an excuse, but merely as a statement of fact.

"I guess it's time for me to speak about it. For the first year, his friends were my friends, and his enemies were my enemies. It got so that the only time I could find myself was when I looked into the mirror, and even then I wasn't completely sure. Well, early one evening"— Judith's voice broke and she braced herself—"one evening I was preparing dinner when the phone rang.

"To this day I don't know what it was, but something about the ring startled me and made me jump to the terrible conclusion that there had been a death in the family. It turned out to be not a death, but it was a loss. A very great loss. Terry Burke, a friend of your father's from work, called to tell me that Roy wasn't coming home that night . . . wasn't coming home at all. And I shouldn't call the police or missing persons because Roy had left of his own free will. He wanted it explained that he wasn't even mad. I was a good woman, but that when push came to shove he didn't want marriage, wasn't cut out for it. He just wanted his freedom back. No hard feelings, it was just one of those things. He even made a point to remind Terry to wish me and the baby luck, the very best of luck."

JUDITH TURNED TO gaze out the kitchen window, and for a while both mother and daughter stayed quiet while listening to the melting snow make plop-plop-plopping sounds as the droplets fell one by one into newly formed puddles. But after a while Carla spoke to the back of her mother's head. "You never told me that."

"You know, some things don't improve very much in the telling. Roy didn't even have the guts to tell me face-to-face."

"All the same you should have told me."

Judith slowly turned her gaze back to her daughter. "Really?"

"Mom, I knew you never wanted to talk about it. I've thought a lot about it, but I guess I figured it all wrong. Knowing that you have such a strong will and guessing that he had one, too—well, I thought that you two had one huge hullabaloo of an argument and neither one would give in and so you and he split."

"And now that you do know he left us, does it make any difference?" Judith's eyes examined her daughter's face for signs of disapproval.

Carla shook her head. "I still don't get it. If you were

so meek and mild when Dad was around, then how could you become so damn fearless after he had gone away? I mean, after all of the responsibility suddenly became only your responsibility?"

Judith's laugh echoed with sadness, as though the joke was on her. "Please don't ever call me 'fearless,' Carla."

"I'm trying to give you a compliment."

Judith's eyes played momentarily on her daughter before answering. "Not when it feels as though you don't know me at all."

"I didn't exactly mean 'fearless,' " she said, accepting the correction. "I know you *feel* fear—I only meant that you don't let fear stand in your way. You just go charging ahead and do whatever needs doing."

Judith gave her daughter a that's-more-like-it nod. "And may I add that that 'charging ahead' quality didn't happen immediately. It evolved slowly, but I don't know if it would have ever happened at all if it hadn't been for you."

The girl managed to look both delighted and quizzical all at the same time. "Because of me? Are you kidding?"

"I remember it so well. More than fifteen years have passed, but it's as fresh in my memory as bread hot from the oven. I was sitting in the wicker rocking chair, rocking you off to sleep, and not any differently than I had rocked you to sleep so many countless times before. There was certainly a difference that time; only the difference wasn't with you; it was with me.

"As you lay sleeping in my arms, I began talking to you, telling you how sorry ... how very sorry I was that I hadn't provided you with a real, in-residence Daddy, but right there and then I made you this promise: You were going to, at the very least, have a mother. I would see to that. You were going to have a real, live mother, somebody that stood for something. Somebody whom you could look up to and hold on to. From that moment on I was determined to become much more than a smudged Xerox copy of the never-to-return Roy Wayland."

Chapter 6

WHEN THE FRONT doorbell chimed, Judith jumped up from the kitchen table while glancing at her watch. "Good Lord, why does that man do that to me?"

"Early Eddie strikes again," sang out Carla. She made it her business to go to the front door. She knew that her mother would appreciate a little time to make sure she was looking her best before her afternoon date with Edward Landis Jameson, III.

Carla swung open the door and was totally surprised. It wasn't the expected Eddie Jameson at all, but a most unexpected Andy Harris, posed nonchalantly on the front porch. "Merry Christmas," he said, handing her a less-than-professionally wrapped gift the size of a pound box of candy. "Oh, my God!" she said, staring at the box as though it were fixing to explode.

"What's the matter, don't you like candy?"

"No, I love candy!" she protested. "I really do! And thank you—it's so nice of you . . . really."

"Are you on a diet?" he asked suspiciously. "You don't need to be on a diet—your figure is great."

The girl took in the compliment without responding. She always found compliments a lot like medicine in capsule form, just too damn difficult to swallow. It wasn't even that she thought the compliment giver was insincere; no, not insincere, but invariably she thought the person mistaken. If she found compliments difficult to accept and even harder to acknowledge, that certainly wasn't true of criticism.

But because this was a compliment, she instinctively dropped her gaze. "No, I'm not on a diet—I didn't mean to act so strange either. It's just that I wasn't expecting you. I never dreamed we were going to exchange gifts so I don't have anything for you. Oh, I wish . . . I really wish I had something for you. . . ."

"Hey, it's no big deal, this is only a box of candy," he said, slipping off his buttery-brown leather jacket before making himself comfortable on the pillow-accentuated sofa. "Besides, seeing you is the best thing that's happened to me all day."

Hearing him say that made her realize that she should trust her instincts because when she first swung open her front door she'd thought that Andy looked a little sad. "Don't tell me that Santa skipped your house?"

"Nah, wait till you see! Dad bought me real professional boxing gear, two sets of gloves, two punching bags. It's not that I don't like the stuff either, it's just that I hate sparring with my dad."

"How come?" Carla looked as surprised as she sounded.

Andy examined her eyes and it wasn't until he found

sufficient understanding there that he felt encouraged enough to continue. "With him, it's not a game, it's a life-or-death struggle, know what I mean?"

Suddenly, beneath his right eye she observed a barely noticeable (but still and all, noticeable) puffiness. "Why, that's ridiculous! He has a huge weight advantage over you!" The girl's voice spilled over with heartfelt outrage that someone would hurt her Andy. "Not to mention arm reach!"

Because her anger acted like a soothing balm for the injustice done him, he smiled appreciatively. "Boy, I wish you'd tell him that! He knocked the living hell out of me and every time I duck, or take a step backwards, he calls me names."

Carla frowned. "Calls you names?"

Andy frowned, too. "Yeah, names!"

"The name calling bothers you as much as the pummeling?" she inquired.

"More! 'Cause he calls me . . ." Andy shook his head, as though it were too painful to speak those names.

"I'll never tell anyone," she offered. "I promise you; it'll be our secret."

"He calls me 'Miss Andy' like I'm some fag!" His face had now taken on a warmish-reddish hue. "Well, I'm not, and he better watch out, too, 'cause the next time we box, I'm going to knock his fucking teeth down his fucking throat! Honest I will!"

"Oh, come on," she said, leaning ever-so-slightly against him. "That's the last thing, the very last thing that anyone could think about you."

He grinned shyly while exhaling what seemed to be a really huge surplus of pent-up hostility.

"Here," she said, presenting the now-opened box of chocolates for his first pick. "Eat something sweet and be reminded that everything in this world isn't sour."

"Well, you're not at all sour, or bitter either, that's for sure. Uh, there was a card that came with the candy."

She began searching through the ribbon and wrappings. "I'm sorry. I didn't see a card."

"You won't find it there," he said shyly, sliding a white card from his shirt pocket. "It's here, and I wrote it just for you."

Taking the card from between Andy's fingers, she began to read aloud:

> Not just today but all the years through
> My heart will always be close to you.
>   Love and kisses,
>   Andy

Leaning forward, she shyly placed a kiss upon his lips. Somewhere between the kissing and the clinging she came to understand that however much she needed him, he needed her more. Quite a bit more!

The door chimed and Andy looked startled, as though his father had tracked him down to challenge him to another till-death-do-us-part boxing match. "It's just my mother's friend," Carla explained while rising to her feet. "He's taking us out for a drive—would you like to join us?"

In the next moments a radiant and rested Judith breezed through the living room to greet Eddie Jameson with a hug, made the introductions, and extended to Andy the same invitation that Carla had. Andy smiled with genuine pleasure.

"Uncle Mark, Aunt Caroline, and their three girls are having Christmas dinner with us today at two. If I don't show up, they'd murder me!"

Judith and Eddie laughed. Judith suggested that nobody's company was worth getting murdered for, "not even Carla's."

As Andy slid his arms into his jacket, he looked at Carla with an expression that she read as regret, regret that he couldn't spend more time with her. Carla felt that their relationship had already deepened and she was certain that Andy felt the same way that she did. "Walk me to my car?"

Outside the sun was brightly shining and the temperature hovered around the freezing mark, which is about as cold as it usually got in Rachetville.

"Oh, by the way," he exclaimed, snapping his fingers. "I saw you and your mother at my church today."

"Oh, yes," Carla responded while making a mental note to pray tonight for forgiveness for the lie that would now be leaving her lips. "Mom and I really liked it there, too. And your preacher is exactly like you said he'd be, dynamic. Really dynamic."

"Boy, you won't believe how right he is, too. Remember what his sermon was about today? Remember how he showed us example after example of what's happening today in the real world and how Satan goes on getting bolder and bolder? Well, you won't believe—you'll never believe just how right that was!"

"Tell me, Andy, what happened?"

"Those queers—one's name is Frank Montgomery and the other is Stephan Jones, the same ones that were prancing around our store until my dad and Claude Hudgins's wife told them where to get off— well, you'll never guess where they went today!"

The girl shook her head as though she didn't have a clue when, in fact, she had not only spotted the two men leaving church, but she had also done something she didn't have the courage to admit: She had smiled when she caught their eye. Even so, she continued to shake her head, because she knew that Andy wouldn't want to hear anything about that.

His face flushed as he shook his fist. "Those filthy fags with their stupid faces sticking out had the nerve to march right into *our* church!" His lips, his lovable lips in front of her very eyes became ugly and sneering. "Why, you'd think they owned the joint!"

Carla felt as though the right side of her body was ripping itself away from the left and soon there would be two separate but equal halves. One of those halves wanted to defend the men because she really liked them. She just felt they were nice, gentle people who wouldn't hurt others. In her heart, she knew that it was the right thing to do. But the other part of her wanted to stand by her man no matter what damn fool thing he said or did. After all, suddenly she felt she belonged—she knew she was Andy's girlfriend. Right or wrong, it was the womanly and loving thing to do since Andy would expect that behavior. Wouldn't that draw Andy and her that much closer together? Didn't she want to be a couple more than anything else?

"What we have to always remember," he sermonized, allowing his voice to rise half-again higher than ordinary conversational level, "is that these are no small sins like stealing apples and telling white lies. This is the vilest sin that a person can commit. Period! Exclamation point! Leviticus twenty-thirteen says it and so does Romans one, twenty to thirty-two."

He paused long enough to give Carla time to throw sweet word bouquets at his feet and at his conclusions. When she didn't offer anything other than silent concentration, he came right out and asked if she didn't feel the same way about fags that he did.

She breathed in deep, taking in breath enough to push out the words. "The reason I'm not saying anything, Andy, is because I don't exactly understand how you can be as religious as you say you are and still . . . still hate. I mean, I'm no big expert on the Bible or anything, but I do know that Jesus was real big on love. He even taught us to love our enemies. Remember him saying that?"

"He didn't mean fags!"

"Oh, come on, Andy," she chided. "You know better than that! Aren't you at least a little afraid that hating can keep you out of heaven? I'm not as religious as you are, but well, I do know some things."

His lips thinned out in silent defiance. "No, absolutely not! What you do or don't do in this life isn't all that important."

"Not important?" Carla repeated.

"Not really," he said confidently. "You could be Adolf Hitler and put millions of people to death in gas chambers, and you'd still have life eternal if . . . if in your last breath, you called on Jesus to wash away your sins, and he'd do it, too. And that means that you'd receive salvation, and once you've got that then you've really got it made 'cause that means that you can spend eternity doing only nice things like chumming around with God." Then after a pause, he added, "Now do you understand?"

"Yes," she answered. "I guess so, but still and all, it doesn't seem right."

Chapter 7

AT PRECISELY 9:25 A.M. on the seventeenth day of January, the national weather service in Little Rock sent out a bulletin saying that a freak ice storm would be passing through the region around noon. Spencer Matson, the superintendent of schools for Rachetville, made his announcement over the speaker system: ". . . so let's get everybody home before the streets become as slippery as cooked okra. But please, please go only as quickly as safety permits. Okay, boys and girls, school is dismissed."

Andy, with a book-filled backpack slung jauntily over one shoulder, raced for Rachetville High's front door as though it had been years and years since he had tasted that delicious morsel called freedom. Following close behind were his two best buddies, Doug "the Ironman" Crawford and Mike "the Spider" Horten. They were chanting in unison: "Pizza and beer! Pizza and beer! Pizza and beer!"

Since you couldn't buy a bottle of beer in Rachetville if your very life depended upon it, it was clear to every student, as well as to every faculty member who heard their chant, that these guys were going to be heading to that livelier, albeit more sinful, place seven miles down the highway.

Ten minutes later, the three crowded together on the front seat of the Harrises' Oldsmobile and drove down Parson Springs's Main Street. Ahead on the right was the venerable Queen Anne Hotel, and five doors farther up was the newest business in town—The Forgotten Treasures Antique Shop.

Once inside the shop a person found herself in the center of a virtual symphony of memorabilia, collectibles, and pure whimsy. A Victorian bird cage held a clay pot with cascading English ivy. In a corner stood a brass lamp with a leaded-glass shade—a grandfather clock with brass finials—a folding teak deck chair with a brass plate on its back reading "Ile de France." An old-style manikin with a painted mustache wearing a gray tunic with heavy gold epaulets, once proudly worn by a long-forgotten Confederate captain during the War between the States.

Frank Montgomery shook his head emphatically at his customer, a young woman with enough carats in her wedding ring to buy an affordable house or two. "Oh, no, you don't want to do that! The Canton vase is too . . . too ordinary for your elegant living room, Karen. Go with the Imari. Definitely, the Imari!"

But as soon as the sale had been made and the customer left the shop happily carrying her nineteenth-century Japanese vase safely encased in Styrofoam peanuts, Frank underwent a radical change, a change from quietly dignified to noisily exuberant. He walked briskly around a Chippendale table set with silver candlesticks and antique Waterford to swing open the door to the rear workshop. Inside, his partner was a study in concentration as he painstakingly replaced the worn, torn, and brittle leather writing surface of a nineteenth-century English writing box.

Waving the white sales slip high in the air, Frank bellowed, "Guess what!?" But before Stephan had even looked up, Frank was already answering his own question. "Know that Omari vase that everybody turned their nose up at when we were on Beacon Hill? Well, let's hear a big round of applause for genial Frank Montgomery 'cause it's been sold at long last. We're rich . . . or at the very least we're bucks and bucks ahead of the bill collector."

"Good show, partner. What did you do, charm the socks off some rich old biddy?"

"Hell no!" replied Frank, sounding as though he were filling up with righteous indignation. "Only thing I did was to charm the socks off some rich young biddy!" To celebrate their victory, they decided to eat a good meal, drink a little wine, and make merry over lunch right in the shop.

Stephan asked what he wanted to eat, and Frank answered, "Surprise me." When Stephan asked what he wanted to drink, Frank again responded, "Surprise me." With only these admittedly wide parameters, Stephan slipped his down jacket over his varnish-stained plaid shirt and sprinted all the way down Main Street to Wayno's Liquor Store, where he bought a bottle of cheap wine imported from Portugal.

Then he headed toward Jimmy Joe's Bar-B-Que Restaurant, where the pork was smoked in pits and anyone who took even one bite understood that here at last was barbecued food that tasted exactly the way God intended it to taste.

When Stephan lived in Boston he was under the crazy impression that he knew exactly what barbecued food was: a glob of sauce from a bottle that made meat taste as though it had been globbed with sauce from a bottle. But now that he was becoming a true-blue Arkansan, he realized at long last how very little he had known. As soon as he entered the small, savory-smelling storefront restaurant, he saw that the take-out line was at least twice as long as usual. Over the take-out window was a sign pencil-written on lined notebook paper: "Sorry we have short hands today 'cause of the ice storm that is a-coming so please be patient."

Stephan smiled at the sign and thought how lucky for Jimmy Joe that he was so great at cooking, because the chance that anyone would ever pay him for his writing was at least a zillion times less than zero. But the next thing he thought was that he didn't have time to waste standing in line, not with all the refinishing, regluing, and restoring waiting for him back at the shop. So, in spite of the fact that the barbecue was a near work of art, he decided to go where the food might not be all that good, but at least he could get it good and quick.

Inside the Pizza Pad, the aroma of tomato sauce and oregano captured the senses. That, along with the unbridled cheers from three high school seniors playing an obviously engrossing electronic fight game.

"A large mushroom and olive pizza with extra cheese and a couple of bags of chips to go please," Stephan called out to a guy wearing a uniform with the red lettering, CHRIS over his right pocket.

As he waited for his order, shifting his weight from his right leg to his left and back again, Stephan chided himself for not thinking to bring along the *Little Rock Gazette,* which was delivered six mornings a week to the shop. It always gave his spirits a special boost when he read that the Boston Celtics or the New England Patriots had actually won one; but when he was forced to read about one of their losses, well, it just hung a kind of pit-of-the-stomach gloom over his whole day. No, he thought, it was probably just as well he had not brought the paper along. Stephan wandered over to watch the action at one of the video games, where two full-color cartoonish characters in a ring were relentlessly slugging the living computer chips out of each other. "Block him, Spider! Block! Block! To the head!" young male voices called out encouragingly to the lean and lanky kid who groaned and grunted over the simulated excitement of the video.

"Hey! Hey! Well, well, looky who's here!" said a voice inches from Stephan's ear. He turned his head and without meaning to—and certainly without wanting to—he let his jaw drop. Glaring at him was that sneering guy from the hardware store. Andy Harris smiled at Stephan Jones from only one corner of his mouth. "Hey . . . how you getting along, ol' buddy?"

Stephan nodded his head. "Oh, okay thanks," he mumbled as he retreated back to the counter just in time to see a golden pizza lavishly sprinkled with black olive slices emerge triumphantly from the oven.

As Stephan, with boxed pizza in hand, closed the door of the store behind him, he wondered how it was possible for the weather to change so dramatically in the fifteen minutes that he had been inside. Now the sky was an icy, glassy blue, and it was almost as though God were playing the role of a great scenic designer in the sky. One glance heavenward and anyone could quickly understand that the entire celestial stage was being readied for some epic event.

When did the streets become so totally deserted? Had everybody already made it home before the approaching ice storm? The heat of the pizza penetrated the bottom of the paper box and Stephan wondered if he wasn't carrying the world's most flavorful hand warmer.

"Hey, you—hey, wait up a sec!" called out Andy as he, the Ironman, and the Spider lumbered briskly toward him. Stephan gave a half-turn, just enough to catch sight of who was calling to him, but instead of stopping, if anything he quickened his pace. "You know, that's not very nice," said Andy, galloping up with his posse. "Hey, don't you know I kind of thought you were more friendly than that. After all, you did come to my church for Christmas services. So how come you came to my church?"

"I've got to get back to work now," Stephan explained, as Andy and the Ironman, who could double as a human wall, barred his way. The Spider sandwiched him in from behind as though he were nothing more than a piece of luncheon meat haphazardly thrown between a couple of slices of bread. "Look, I've got to go. . ." Stephan pleaded. "I'm already late."

"Now, now, you don't have to be like that 'cause I just want to introduce you to my friends, Mike the Spider Horten and Doug the Ironman Crawford, here," Andy said with disarming sweetness.

"But, say, I am sorry, but I don't really remember your name."

Stephan's head drooped, but his answer came out clear enough. "Stephan."

"Stephan?" mocked the double-sized Ironman. "Stephan! What kind of a fruititooti name is that?"

"Hey, now don't go ridiculing a man's name, Ironman," Andy interjected. "A man's home is his castle and a man's name is his castle, too. Or something like that."

Ironman and Spider laughed appreciatively. "Yeah, so *where* did you get such a fruititooti faggy name as Stephan?" Spider asked in a voice so deep that it seemed downright misplaced in so tall and spidery a guy. This time it was Andy and Ironman who laughed raucously.

When Stephan didn't immediately respond, Andy gave him a shove backward. "Answer the man!" he yelled, as Spider gave their captive an even harder shove forward. "What's the matter with you anyway, don't you believe in being polite?"

"Leave me alone," Stephan begged with a voice that trembled. "Am I bothering you? I'm not bothering you!"

"That's where you're wrong—you—you fucking fag!" Andy shouted, giving him a two-handed shove so unexpectedly violent that both Stephan and his backstop, Spider, went stumbling backwards. Spider lost his footing and sprawled against the concrete sidewalk. When Andy extended a hand to his fallen comrade, Stephan faked to the right and took off running to the left, still carrying the pizza in one hand and the Portuguese wine in the other. He sprinted down the empty street as though this were one race he had to win.

Footsteps heavily pounding the pavement, down-up, down-up, in rapid-fire succession came behind him. Stephan knew he could run faster and harder than his two thick-bodied tormentors. But what about the other one? The one built like a willow reed? What about him!?

Suddenly Stephan was grabbed by the sleeve of his down jacket and spun crazily around. The pizza and wine went crashing to the asphalt. Strong arms from behind encircled his neck like a tightening vise. The willow reed had him! Pressing hard, pressing hard against his Adam's apple. Air! Air! He began gagging at the same time that he silently screamed for air.

In the next moments, the other two surrounded him. The steel neck-hold was released, and air, blessed air rushed once again to fill his lungs. "Good work, Spider!" complimented Andy. "Grab those hands—hold them behind his back, Ironman!"

Shaking his head in disgust, Andy surveyed the debris from the shattered wine bottle as he made *tsk-tsk-tsk*ing sounds with the tip of his tongue. "Boy, you got some nerve messing up the street, you really do, Stephan— Stephan-*eeee*. That is your name, isn't it, Stephanie?"

Stephan swallowed and wondered how come it hurt so much to swallow. Then Andy latched on to his cheeks, one in each of his hands, and began pulling them outward until the groaning man's face took on hideous proportions. "When I speak to you—you answer me! Understand, fruit fly?"

"Yes," Stephan answered in a hoarse whisper. "Yes."

"Now that's much better," Andy beamed triumphantly while bending over to pick up the fallen box of pizza.

"It's still good enough to eat," the Ironman observed with what sounded like near reverence. "And hot, too."

"Well in that case," Andy proclaimed while carefully removing it from the box, "let Stephanie eat it!" He smashed the still steamy pizza hard against Stephan's face.

"AWWWLLL!" screamed Stephan, slapping the scalding cheese from his cheeks. The tormentors, frightened by the sounds of anguish that filled the streets, took off running; so did the tormented, only in the opposite direction.

Less than three minutes later, a single sleigh bell jangled as the door of Forgotten Treasures was opened and then slammed shut. Wearing a decidedly annoyed expression, Frank Montgomery looked up from the display case he was rearranging. "It's about time! A man could starv—My God, Stevie, what's wrong!?"

Biting hard on his lower lip to keep his emotions from spilling over, Stephan Jones rushed straight through the store. Whizzing wordlessly by his dumbfounded partner, he ran into the workshop and to the sink. He turned the spigot on full volume and began bathing his singed face with cold water.

Nervously Frank hovered over him. "You're as red as a beet! What in God's name happened!? How did your face get burned? You know, we better go to the emergency room, let them check you out."

Stephan tore some paper towels from the roll and began to wet them under the tap before pressing them gently to his face. "No, it's better now . . . really."

With words so heavy that they seemed almost weighted, Frank asked, "You going to tell me who did this to you?" Then he listened as he heard a rush of air race through Stephan's nostrils en route to his lungs. It was as though he needed the extra supply of oxygen just to help himself push out the story.

"From the hardware store over in Rachetville. That young punk. He and his two friends."

"Oh, yes." Frank's forehead wrinkled up like an old washboard. "That's the little bastard and his family that preacher tried to introduce us to at Christmas services?"

His partner closed his eyes as he pressed the cold, wet paper towels against his face. "That's the one."

Frank's eyes registered concern as he nodded slowly. "All right, we'll talk later. Look, I'm going to run across the street to Dyer's Drug and buy some ointment or something to put on your face—maybe an ice bag, too. Yeah, an ice bag would be good."

As soon as Stephan Jones heard the tinkling front door of the shop close behind Frank, his tightly buttoned-down mouth burst wide open, and then his slender body began to tremble uncontrollably as he cried out with equal parts fury, frustration, and pain.

Chapter 8

AT PRECISELY SIX o'clock in the evening, the tortoiseshell Tiffany mantel clock began eloquently chiming out the hours. Dripless candles in brass candlesticks illuminated the faces of the two men who sat stiffly at opposite ends of the golden oak dining table. The only consistent sound was the sound of the flatware as it cut and scraped against the porcelain dinner plates. But every so often either one or the other made an attempt at conversation that drifted off into nothingness.

The one ingredient that was unmistakably there was gloom. Frank was trying hard, way too hard, in fact, to keep Stephan's spirits up. And Stephan was pretending much too hard that his spirits were already up.

When, for example, Frank told a joke and Stephan laughed uproariously, Frank caught on that they were both merely pretending, and neither was doing a particularly good job of fooling the other. "You know, you didn't laugh half that hard the first time I told you that joke," he observed.

"The reason for that," Stephan retorted while smiling his first genuine smile of the evening, "is that the first time I heard it, I didn't have to pretend that I was having fun."

Suddenly Frank snapped his fingers and, presto, that worried look he had been previously wearing was replaced by a wraparound grin.

"Know what we need?" he asked, and without waiting for Stephan to do more than look surprised, he began answering his own question. "A vacation! We've been working around the clock since we left Boston. We need a long weekend away from these small-town bigots with their mindless ways."

Stephan sighed. "Hmm, a weekend away ... maybe that would give us a better perspective. Help us see that this place isn't out to get us, 'cause one of our problems is that we're taking those three stooges too seriously."

Frank slapped his hands together and made a whooping sound. "We could close early Friday and drive to Little Rock, stay in one of those new hotels with an indoor swimming pool."

"An indoor pool?" Stephan asked, at the same time managing to look as though he'd never before heard of such a crazy thing. "Why do we need an indoor pool? You know I hate pools."

"Well, this may come as a shock to your nervous system, Stevie, but people have been known to like to swim in them."

Stephan shook his head no. "You know I don't—I can't—I don't want to. We've been together long enough for you to accept the fact that you like to swim and I won't ... ever."

"Are you *serious*? You *really* can't swim?" Frank threw up his hands. "Okay, so no big deal. Let me teach you—did I ever tell you that I was on the Boston College swim team?"

"Too many times. But listen, get yourself another disciple 'cause I don't want to learn."

"It's easy," Frank insisted. "I can have you swimming in thirty minutes—fifteen minutes, guaranteed!"

"No thanks."

"What do you mean 'no thanks.' Can't you hear when opportunity's pounding on your door?"

Stephan jumped out of his chrome and wicker chair and glared daggers at him from across the table. "Can't you for once in your life get off my case? To say that I've had a tough day would be a vast understatement. What in the hell do I need you carping at me for!? And if I had wanted to learn to swim, don't you think I would have learned long before now—well, don't you?!"

Frank threw his hands up in a don't-shoot-'cause-I-surrender gesture. "Hey, hey, slow down, Stevie, I'm sorry I upset you . . . so just let it go, okay?"

Stephan dropped back down into his chair and allowed his shoulders to droop forward as though a terrible fatigue had suddenly overtaken him. "I didn't mean to jump down your throat. It's just that I. . ."

"Forget it," answered Frank, flipping his hand as though it were a thing of little consequence. "I understand."

"No, you don't!" contradicted Stephan. "How could you? I'm embarrassed—ashamed even to admit this to you, but, you see, I've never learned how to swim. I'm afraid to learn because . . . well, I'm afraid, deathly afraid, of water."

Chapter 9

THE FIRST WEEK of March was also something of a first for Judith Wayland—she had at last inaugurated a new program at the Rachetville Public Library that was very much talked about, but was not one bit controversial. Because most tests at the junior and senior high schools were scheduled for Monday, she kept the library open until midnight every Sunday and invited volunteer tutors in math, science, history, and English to be available to help the students. As a kind of bonus to all the young scholars and their tutors, at nine o'clock, peanut butter sandwiches and orange juice were available free to all in the staff lounge.

Even though Carla was sitting between Debby and Andy at the oak library table, she was, for the most part, still able to concentrate on her thousand-word composition due Monday for language arts: "Do you believe that Patty Bergen in *Summer of My German Soldier* did the moral thing in hiding a German prisoner?"

Feeling something hitting her foot, she moved it out of the way, but the only thing she received for her trouble was a second, slightly more insistent kick. Glancing up she found herself peering straight into the Aegean-blue eyes of Andy. "Wanta go outside with me, Carla?" he asked, combing back his own burnished brown hair with his slender fingers.

Although her first thought was that she'd gladly follow him to places farther away and more exotic than merely the front steps of the public library, she did regret being diverted from her writing just when she had a really good rhythm going. "I'll be back in a few minutes, Debby," she informed her friend. She took off her glasses and tossed them on top of her loose-leaf notebook.

For the last nine and a half weeks now, Carla had thought almost exclusively about Andy and their developing relationship and had come to the conclusion that they were settling down and settled in because, at least, now the *big* issue had been settled.

It happened on New Year's Eve amid some heavy petting and even heavier panting. Andy yelped, "If you love me, *really* love me, you'll let me do it. All the way!"

They had been seeing each other every day and every evening since Christmas. Carla had anticipated that the issue would come up and she had settled it in her own head first.

Putting everything into the equation—should she or shouldn't she—Carla had finally pared it all down to the essentials: If she couldn't control her biology, how could she control her destiny? Could she live with the consequences of becoming pregnant? So by the time Andy's challenge was thrown at her, she knew precisely what she was going to say, and she said it: "If you love me, Andy, *really* love me, you wouldn't ask."

Outside on the well-lit steps there was a cool breeze blowing up from the west, and Carla was glad she had remembered to slip into her cardigan sweater before walking out into the night.

As she turned, she caught sight of his shadow against the library wall just as it descended toward her. His cheek touched hers, and she closed her eyes while taking in his manly warmth and wondered how it could be that he always smelled so *hmmm* good, as though he had just stepped out of a long, hot shower. Gently laying her hands on his cheeks, she brought his face to her face and her lips to his lips.

The kiss resonated through her body and, if she wasn't mistaken, she even felt a tingling sensation all the way down to the arches of her feet. "There," the girl murmured, moving her head just far enough away so as to better gauge his reaction. "You know, you're a pretty wonderful fellow. Sometimes it's hard to believe that you really care for me."

Andy smiled shyly, which made him look different. Maybe his smile made him look younger, but at any rate it certainly made him look a lot less assured. "I feel that way, too. I guess I'm surprised that you"—he looked down to examine his fingernails—"that you care for me, too."

"Really?" Carla was all ears.

"Well, sure . . ."

"Funny, that's not the way you act," she teased, but in all seriousness. "Mostly you act like—like you're God's gift to women!"

He pulled her close, "Oh, be nice, pretty lady."

Carla checked out Andy's face for the slightest sign of fraud, but she found none. How could that be? How could that possibly be, she mused, that he could call her pretty? Because no matter how many different mirrors she had gazed into in how many different places, she never once saw anything staring back at her that even remotely resembled beauty. Was it, she wondered, because others could see what she could not? Or was it that she, only she, could fathom deep beneath her seemingly seamless surface, down deep where the formless fears and cowardly confusions soundlessly churned on.

"C'mon," he said walking hand in hand with her toward the public telephone booth that stood in front of the library. "Time for me to do a little prank."

Carla groaned. "Oh, for God's sake, Andy! You're not going to do what I think you are? It's getting close to midnight."

"Hey, what's the matter with you anyway?" Andy said. "How come you *never* like to have any fun?"

Andy's remark struck Carla with more force than he realized, partly because he had eventually accepted her wishes and stopped hounding her for sex—for serious you-could-have-a-baby sex, that is. Wasn't that another reason that she should do everything else to please him? Didn't he deserve no less?

Beneath her feet, the girl felt the high moral ground begin to shift. Am I making much too much out of all of this? she wondered. One thing, at least, was becoming clear: Her mother's lofty idealism had been far more contagious than she had imagined. And not just more contagious, but also a hell of a lot more inconvenient than she'd have liked it to be.

What is this anyway? She tried to talk herself into excusing him. Just a bit of stupid boyish fun. No harm done! Besides, if it really were wrong wouldn't Andy, being as religious as he was, be the first to realize it? After all, he was not merely a churchgoer, he also faithfully watched some of the most dynamic preachers in the world on cable television. Everybody who heard him was awfully impressed how he could go on and on quoting Reverend Wheelwright or Jerry Falwell. So with all that religion how could Andy Harris be anything but good?

Probably even the pestered men themselves didn't take it all that seriously, at least not nearly as seriously as she did! What was wrong with her anyway? Those guys weren't her friends. Andy was the one she wanted, she needed. Only had he brought her into the fold, making her belong.

But maybe it was already too late. Maybe she had already gone and blown it because Andy had probably already come to the conclusion that she was just another tight-assed prude with a thou-shalt-not-have-any-fun personality! She made a conscious effort to lighten up. "Well, okay, if you want to make a prank call go ahead. Only don't say anything nasty—please."

With repugnance, Carla noticed how his pace quickened to double time as he approached the pay phone. Dropping a coin in the slot, he began dialing the number that had obviously been committed to memory. After the third ring went unanswered, she felt a growing sense of relief because chances were the men were somewhere other than home. In the middle of the fourth ring, the chances of that happening dropped to zero.

Andy held the receiver in his right fist as tightly as any lethal weapon.

"Good evening, Frank," Andy said, sounding strangely pleasant. "I just called to find out how your little boyfriend liked his pizza, huh? What terrible table manners, getting food all over himself! Gross!"

Considering what he had just heard, Frank's response was surprisingly cool. "Please explain to me," he began, "what kind of men would gang up three to one against one perfectly peaceful guy going about his own business?"

Andy's voice boomed. "Who do you think you're talking to, you fucking fruit fly!"

"Actually, I had thought that my question had given even you enough clues to be able to figure that one out for yourself." Then Frank sighed as though having to explain really primary stuff to idiots was both physically and emotionally draining. "But if you still need help with it, then I'm prepared to make it simple enough for you to understand."

Andy squealed like a stuck pig. "Who do you think you're talking to—you—you queer pervert!"

"Sad to say it, I'm wasting time talking to you! Someone who may be as strong as a man, and as tall as a man, but there the resemblance abruptly ends! For you are not a man, little boy! Because what you are is a genuine, one hundred percent, certified coward!"

Even with only the light from the street lamp, Carla could tell that Andy's jawline had hardened into granite while his face had taken on a really rosy hue. As his lips pressed against the receiver he screeched, "You better take that back, you hear me! Cause I'll get you for that!"

Suddenly there was a great bang as though the phone at the other end of the line had crashed against a hard and immovable object. Grabbing his ear while groaning in pain, Andy then heard that decisive click that disconnected him from the one person in this world who he hated beyond reason. Andy shouted into the disconnected line. "I swear to God on Jesus' holy name that if it's the last thing I ever do you're going to get it!"

Chapter 10

ON MONDAY MORNING, Debby's predictable chime of the Wayland doorbell made Carla jump to her feet. "See you later, Mom," she said, gathering up her books and making a smacking sound that very nearly made contact with Judith's cheek.

There was rarely anything that resembled an actual greeting between Carla and Debby. Through years of practice they easily picked up the threads of conversation where they had left them minutes or hours or even days before. And there certainly wasn't a greeting now as Debby pushed her oversized glasses back on her nose while flatly stating, "You know, the more I think about it, the more I think I'd be making a serious mistake going into nursing when I could spend almost the same amount of time in college and become a veterinarian."

"Not only that," added Carla enthusiastically, "a vet

is so much more you! You wouldn't have to take orders from a lot of doctors—and you *know* how much you love to take orders."

Debby flashed a smile, rewarding Carla for so well understanding. "I sure do wish you loved animals as much as I do. We could be vets together."

"It's not that I don't love animals," Carla protested. "It's just that I love children more. After I get my degree in early childhood education from the University of Arkansas, I want to work and someday I'll have my own day-care center. Know what else I'm going to do? Teach parents how to take better care of their kids."

Carla wanted to talk about something else—about someone she cared about very much and yet was causing her great concern. Particularly when that someone acted with such unreasonable hatred.

Among the many things that Carla admired about Debby was her ability to dive head-on into heavy waters. But for herself, Carla was more comfortable easing in one teeny-weeny toe at a time. "Notice how upset Andy was when he drove us home from the library last night?"

"You all have a fight?"

"No, but maybe I wouldn't have felt so mad at myself this morning if we had!"

"You going to tell me what happened?" Debby asked.

"Andy is leading a crusade against a couple of antique dealers in town. They're the two gay guys I told you about—you know, the ones who were in Harris's that day."

"Yeah, but what business is that of Andy's?"

Carla shrugged. "Beats me. Ever since one of the men was overheard saying something loving it got

Andy crazy that two guys are like that. He's been hassling them or else talking about hassling them. One or the other."

Debby shook her head decisively. "Andy shouldn't be doing that." And just those simple words—"Andy shouldn't be doing that"—could be ammunition enough, thought Carla, to supply her with the courage to look into his bottomless blue eyes and tell him straight out: "What you're doing is wrong!"

Carla began to imagine the scene. Maybe she'd take Andy's hand before leading him to a place where they could truly be alone. To her favorite spot in all of Rachetville, a grassy stretch along the east bank of the Pascaloosa River. This time her mission would be very different, because this time she couldn't just lazily daydream. With all the conviction she could express, she'd come right out and tell him, "I really, really hate it when you're hating. I hate it even more when you try to force me into hating, too!"

But when it was Andy's turn to respond, her clear mental image of the scene began to blur, gradually fading into a fogginess that made Carla's vision as obscure as a moonless night. Again and again she struggled to conjure up just the right daydream, the one that had him anguished over the pain that he had caused, so anguished, in fact, that he promised never again to give in to hatred.

But again and again the girl's repeated attempts at visualizing Andy's remorse failed. No matter how hard she tried, from whatever angle she looked, she simply could not "see" him feeling even a penny's worth of pity for someone else's pain. Especially not for the pain he caused Frank Montgomery and Stephan Jones.

* * *

DURING LUNCH, THE Rachetville High School cafeteria had any number of hubs of activity, each one presided over by one or more high-energy individuals. At one of these hubs, Andy Harris, surrounded by Spider, Ironman, and their girlfriends Lisa and Donna, was reading aloud from a letter written on crinkly blue-gray stationery. It was addressed to Frank Montgomery. At first glance, the juvenile scrawl was a bit surprising, particularly since the writer himself was so exceptionally well coordinated.

Andy frowned gravely as he began to read:

Dear Fruit fly—You and your queer pervert boyfriend are not going to get away with PERVERSION! NO WAY! The Apostle Paul said people who do what you do cannot enter into the Kingdom of Heaven! Remember that the Apostle Paul did not say MAYBE you couldn't or PROBABLY you couldn't! He said you could *not*!!! Period!!! Exclamation Point!!! End of Argument!!! You are going to fry like a french fried potato in the hot, humid, stinking, filthy bowels of hell and I'll be GLAD!!! This is a warning to stay out of our town and get out of our Christian state of Arkansas FAST!!! Or take the CONSEQUENCES!!

A(venging) H(ero)

Even before Carla reached their special lunch table, she could hear the whoops and hollers of approval from Andy and the gang. "What's up?" she asked, sliding her lunch tray onto her "reserved" space at the table next to him.

"Oh, wait until you hear the letter he wrote! Dy-na-mite!" chanted Donna, giving each syllable separate but equal emphasis. "Read it again, Andy. Carla has *got* to hear this!"

Carla wondered if Donna began talking that way

after she became a cheerleader or did they make her a cheerleader because she just naturally talked that way?

Proudly Andy slipped the letter out of an envelope with a giant A and a giant H on its upper left-hand corner. This time he began reading the letter for her and her alone. She couldn't help noticing that Donna and Ironman, Spider and Lisa, all had their eyes focused on her.

Was her consistently less than enthusiastic bashing of Frank and Stephan a matter of the group's concern? she wondered. Before she could be completely accepted in their golden inner circle was it absolutely necessary for her to demonstrate her loyalty to them all by becoming really gung ho, making their enemies *her* enemies?

Andy continued to read with undisguised emotion. "You are not—repeat NOT—going to get away with perversion."

Who appointed Andy Harris moral judge and jury to the world? She felt her own temperature jump even higher as he emphasized the "Fry like a french fried potato" line. What incredible arrogance! Where did he get the idea that God is as cruel and as sadistic to another fellow human being as he is?

Finally, Andy's eyes left the page as he delivered the next line straight from memory. "This is a warning to stay out of our town and get out of our Christian state of Arkansas. FAST!!! Or take the consequences!"

"And I signed it at the bottom with a big A and a big H," Andy added, "so they'd know it was me—but next to the A I spelled out avenging, and next to the H I spelled out hero. So that way they won't be able to prove a thing!"

Upon hearing that, Carla thought that beyond arrogance and cruelty, there was also stupidity. Raw and rank STUPIDITY! Hadn't Andy ever heard of finger-prints and handwriting experts? And the others, what was wrong with them? Just why were they grinning as though they had accidentally discovered the questions to be asked on the history final exam?

"So?" asked Lisa. "Isn't it something? You think those faggots are going to hang around Parson Springs? I know for a fact that they're not going to hang around. Faggots aren't brave people. Ask anyone who knows them—everybody will tell you the same thing, they're not what anyone would call brave!"

Carla looked up into the faces around her, fearful of becoming like them and at the same time, perhaps, even more fearful that she might not be accepted by them. She felt her entire insides silently screaming out for compassion and understanding for two fellow human beings whose only crime was . . . was being different.

"Answer my question already," demanded Andy. "Do you or don't you think my letter is awesome?"

Soundlessly she heard herself scream back her response. "Your letter is disgusting! A disgrace! You should all feel dirty and ashamed, but you Andy Harris, are the leader, and you should feel the most shame of all." That's exactly what she did say in the deepest, quietest, and most real part of her being.

But the voice of audible, hearable sound—the one she depended upon to communicate her approval or dis-approval to a generally disinterested world spoke dif-ferently. "Oh, Andy, are you really going to send this? Aren't you afraid you'll get in trouble?" Sadly she noted that not a single one of her words carried even a touch of the moral outrage that was now exploding within her.

While Andy seemed pleased that he had so much of her concern, he tossed away the question of fear with a quick but determined toss of his head.

Even so it was clear to Carla that he still needed her to express her admiration of his poison pen.

"Here," she announced, taking the letter from his hand. "Better let me read it for myself."

Although the disgust began to well up in her stomach even before her eyes finished scanning the letter, she knew that she couldn't lose him. After all, what did this really have to do with them? With their love for each other? "Wow! This letter is really something!" she boomed. "It's, you know, incredible!"

She waited, half expecting to be struck down by God's own lightning (those special lightning rods he must use for his worst-case hypocrites), or at the very least to be overcome by the hypocrite's strong sense of self-disgust, but strange to say, that's not what seemed to be happening. Because for the first time, she could almost feel those unseen barriers (the ones that had, up to now, been separating her from the others) begin to fall away. Funny, it was kind of funny, but now for the very first time, the whole group was truly united, sharing something as strong and as powerful as hate.

Seeing Andy and his friends visibly warming to her, she understood at long last that to get along sometimes you just had to go along. But if that was true, then how come there was a sad and sickening feeling deep in the hollow of her stomach?

Chapter 11

FRANK SHIFTED THE Winnebago into reverse and began backing away from the garage. Stephan grumbled, "This is ridiculous! Driving the monster to work when we could just as easily take the bikes or walk. We'll never find three consecutive parking places, and even if we do we're practically guaranteed to forget to feed the meters and get tickets." And to make his point even stronger, Stephan flashed the middle three fingers of his right hand. "*Three* tickets!"

Frank backed the recreational vehicle onto leafy Bennett Street. "Boy, you know something? You're as cranky this morning as an old virgin!"

"Well, you'd be cranky, too, Frankie, if you had been wakened from a sound sleep by an obscene and threatening phone call!"

"What do you mean *if*?" Frank loudly demanded, swiveling his head a full ninety degrees to stare with mock disbelief at Stephan. "And exactly where do you think I was when that piece of slime phoned? Sailboating off Marblehead harbor? Or maybe snorkeling in the Cayman Islands?"

Stephan's lower lip pouted out, giving him a cross-little-boy look. "Yeah, but you went right back to sleep, and I didn't!"

Frank shook his head slowly. "Relax, Stevie," he said soothingly. "We just can't take the Andy Harrises of this world too seriously. It reminds me of the summer I visited my grandparents on their farm not far from Richmond, Virginia."

Stephan looked quizzical. "These harassments remind you of your visit to the farm? Pardon me, and not to be nosy, but did I miss something?"

Without paying the slightest attention to his partner's skepticism Frank explained. "As my grandfather and I tramped across the cow pasture, I found myself skipping to the right, jumping to the left, or sometimes merely hopping over piles of manure. All the while Poppy never deviated a millimeter from his straight-line destination.

"By the time we reached the barn, I had inches more manure on my shoes than Poppy. And while he appeared cool and composed, I had enough sweat rolling down my face to water the vegetable garden. When I asked why that was so, he said something that I knew I'd always remember."

"What was that?" asked Stephan, finally engaged.

Frank closed his eyes while rubbing across the deepening lines in his high forehead. " 'Son,' he told me, 'it never does much good to go hopping and skipping just to avoid a little cow dung 'cause there's far too much shit and far too many shitheads in this world for you to avoid them! So my advice to you is to always act like a man and go marching on through.' "

Frank's laugh was deep and rich and every bit as contagious as a case of childhood measles. So contagious, in fact, that in spite of himself Stephan caught it, too.

Frank expertly maneuvered the oversized vehicle into a vacant space in a downtown alleyway. As the men hiked up the narrow, picturesque business street that wound up the mountain, they passed the Ozark Craft Shop, The Two Dumb Dames Fudge Factory, Beau's Leatherworks, Country Cuzzin Quilts, and Gazebo Books. As they walked past Josie's Authentic Mexican Restaurant, they heard someone calling their names.

"Frankie! Stevie! How come you handsome dudes don't come see Josie no more?" shouted out the well-into-middle-age buxom owner, Josie Fernandez Campbell Wicksham O'Brien. "What's the matter, don't you all love me no more?"

As they peered at the woman who leaned languidly against the restaurant's front door, Frank grinned. "Oh, Josie, heart of my heart, are you kidding me? Stevie and I had burritos at your place Thursday."

The cafe owner vigorously shook her head, allowing her freedom-loving hair to bounce off in all conceivable directions. "What good does that do me? I don't want to just *cook* for you. I want to see you, too—sit with you for a spell and tell you about all the many loves of my life. What you think, old women don't like to look at pretty people? That what you think?"

Stephan smiled a genuine, although ever-so-slightly embarrassed smile, while Frank, with a knowing look in his eye, called back, "Josie honey, you're going to be many things, but you're never going to be old, I can promise you that 'cause lady, you're the real thing—you've got that certain . . . spark."

"Spark, is it?" Josie retorted, throwing her hands against her wide waist. "Too bad you fellows weren't around here thirty-five or forty years ago, back when I was young. You think I couldn't *spark* your interest? Light your fires? Well, with a *real* woman like me around you all would be lost to each other and as straight as an arrow. I can tell you that."

With both hands Frank clutched his heart. "Oh, my God," he yelled, shoving Stephan off the granite sidewalk. "Beat it, boy! Oh, it's happening to me, Josie. It's happening to me now." He dropped to one knee. "Finally, true love has struck. Oh, Josie, oh, Josie, it's you!"

Josie snapped the yellow dish towel at her waist at a surprised Frank. "Laugh all you want to, but just remember you don't know what you don't know if you don't know it! Now ain't that so? You just remember to come on back to see me, you heah?"

"Yes ma'am," Frank called out. Laughing, both men headed smartly up winding corkscrewlike Bennett Street toward their shop.

The morning sun was just now peeking over the ridge of the mountain, and they both felt acutely aware of being alive and especially happy to be alive in their funny little, funky little place high in the Arkansas Ozarks. Frank wondered how many places there were where people could come together with nothing more or less to bind them together than the joy of being human. Here in this place it really was true what they said—even the misfits *fit*.

The two felt wrapped in this special privileged glow—until they reached the front door of Forgotten

Treasures, when their bubble of contentment popped and all their warm and wonderful feelings ended with a sudden crash. Across the door and window of their shop, black spray paint sloppily spelled out one seven-letter word: F A G G O T S ! ! !

For several moments, Stephan and Frank wordlessly stood and stared at the desecration, as though ultimately it would dawn on them exactly how and when and why—especially why this would happen here in this lovely and loving mountain village. Finally it was Stephan who broke the silence. "There's at least a quart of turpentine in my workshop. That should do the job."

The offensive graffiti was laboriously turpentined from view, but it could not as easily be wiped from their consciousness. They couldn't even guess at how many days, weeks, or even years it would take for the stain to be similarly scrubbed from their hearts and minds.

At one o'clock in the afternoon, Frank's stomach began growling out the low, angry, roarlike warnings that it needed nourishment, since for all practical purposes, it hadn't been attended to all day. Not unless the not-quite-fresh glazed donut that he had eaten that morning while driving the monster to work counted. Sticking his head into the workshop, he called out, "I'm starved! What's for lunch, Stevie?"

Stephan glanced up from the art deco clock he was rewiring. "There's a hot thermos of bean and barley soup and meat-loaf sandwiches made with whole-wheat bread, romaine lettuce, and Dijon mustard."

Frank and Stephan sat down to steaming bowls of golden-yellow liquid. "Hmm," murmured Frank, taking in the sight and the smell. "What is it about soup that makes it taste even better the second time around?"

"I don't understand you," Stephan flatly announced.

Frank sipped a spoonful of soup before answering. "What's to understand? I'm just your average, every-day, wonderful fellow."

Stephan rested his chin on his fist. "Here we are harassed at home, harassed at work, harassed through the mails, and that's not even taking into account the first-degree burns I suffered, so what do you do? Compliment my cooking!"

Frank threw his friend a look that was every bit as cutting as a chain saw. "Now you just wait up one damn minute! I didn't say I didn't want to do anything, now did I? Think back, the only thing I insisted on this morning was that we shouldn't go rushing off to the police. At least *not* until we calmed down, talked things over, and considered our options. *All* our options."

When Stephan didn't answer, Frank continued. "If you're offended because I can still enjoy food in spite of that wretched graffiti then I'm sorry, but I have no intention of apologizing. Maybe any fool can appreciate and even applaud life when it's perfect, but it takes something extra, *somebody* who has a little something extra, to be able to celebrate life when it's less than perfect."

Stephan nodded his head, allowing his sand-colored hair to bounce up and then down before it finally fell across his forehead. "I guess maybe I was jumping the gun again."

"Yep, guess you sure enough were!" snapped back Frank, who picked up his plastic soupspoon to take another swallow of the steaming, savory stuff. They ate their meal in silence, but it was not the imposed and angry silence of locked-in-battle combatants struggling desperately to score points. Instead it was the self-conscious quiet of people who were a little nervous, that maybe they had gone too far with each other, and yet didn't exactly know how to say they were sorry.

Stephan stood up from his workbench to stretch. "All right, Frank, the ball is in your court. You're so against going the police route; tell me what, if anything, you *are* for?"

"I'm not *so* against going to the police," Frank shot back, hoisting his hundred and ninety-five pounds onto the freshly applied leather writing surface of the roll-top desk. "It's just that I'm uncertain whether we should go to Rachetville and talk with the cops there, since that's where the perpetrators live. Or—and this is the big question—should we explain our situation to the Parson Springs police, since this is where the assault on you and the vandalism of our shop took place."

Stephan snapped his finger just as though the solution, too, was an equally easy snap. "Don't you know that the cops that have the jurisdiction are *our* guys. Besides, the local law is always more sensitive to the human mix in Parson Springs than those redneck yahoo lawmen in Rachetville could ever be."

"Right!" boomed out Frank, pointing a decisive finger in the direction of his partner. "Precisely my point! Just let a member of the police department wearing his lily-of-the-valley shoulder patch drive over to Rachetville to question young Mister Harris and his gang and what you've done is created a bona fide local hero."

"And once that's accomplished," added Stephan, following his partner's logic to its conclusion, "then Andy becomes bolder, recruits more followers, and becomes literally unstoppable."

Together the antique merchants silently bobbed their

heads back and forth in agreement while they seemed to fall deeper and deeper into thought. "Well, what if *their* police handled it?" asked Stephan.

"How do you think they'd *handle* it?"

Stephan shook his head sadly but knowingly. "Considering the fact that one of their cops, Virgil Miller, is rumored to be grand wizard of the Ku Klux Klan, my guess is that Andy and his pals would be given gold medals in the town square while the high school band played 'For He's a Jolly Good Fellow.' "

It was clear from Frank's expressive face as well as the ironic smile that played off the corner of his mouth that he was taking in Stephan's vision and then some. "I can see it now," he interjected. "A gaggle of guys wearing white sheets would be the honor guard for Andy Harris and his gang while there would be a great outpouring of proud townspeople there just to cheer them on."

But just as suddenly as the smile played across his face, it abruptly left. "Forget going to the Rachetville police," Frank said. "The only thing that would accomplish would be to trade three *known* enemies for an entire community of enemies."

"Sounds like our options are narrowing."

Frank nodded thoughtfully. "We could, I suppose, go to the hardware store, try talking with Andy's father."

Stephan forced a sad-sounding chuckle. "Give me a break! Where do you think he learned his hate to begin with? Why not go to the one person who should be able to replace hate with love?" he asked before pausing for a seemingly interminable period.

"For Christ sakes, out with it Stevie!"

"I was thinking . . . what if we went to see the Harrises' minister, Reverend Wheelwright?"

This time Frank's eyebrows jumped halfway to his

hairline. "You don't mean *that* Reverend Wheelwright? Not the Reverend Wheelwright that probably broke the majority of his fist bones while pounding on his pulpit, pleading with his parishioners to join Jesus' army to destroy homosexuals? Surely, goodness and mercy, you certainly can not possibly mean *that* Reverend Wheelwright?"

"Granted. Granted everything you say about him is true. He deserves to be called what he seemed to be in his sermon: a true minister of hate. . . . Still and all," said Stephan, shaking a warning finger in Frank's direction, "still and all, Frankie, what you probably can't fully appreciate is something that I learned at the Weston School of Theology. For the most part, men of the cloth really do want to do the right thing once they come to know what the right thing is. Besides, what he said from the pulpit is not taken all that seriously either by him *or* his congregation. For a minister, there's always two kinds of truth."

Suddenly Frank swung his arm as though he were preparing to lead a mighty cheer. "Hooray for the two kinds of truth! Hooray for the three musketeers. Hooray for the four winds! Hooray for the five walls of the Pentagon! Hooray for the six—"

"All right, Frank! Be cute if you want to, and do what you want to, but do me a favor—leave me out! *Out!*"

"Hey! Hey! Calm down. . . ." Frank advised, while gesturing with his hands in a way that made it look as though he were busily patting down the air. "And you don't have to tell me because I already know it! I talk too much! Comes from my mother's side of the family; it's only my Italian roots showing. I'm always trying to kid even when I should be *trying* to listen."

"Well . . ." said Stephan, filling his lungs with air, "what I was *trying* to say before I was so rudely interrupted is that there are two kinds of truth. Reverend Wheelwright was giving what most everyone in his congregation would understand as merely a Sunday truth. A Sunday truth is something that you might half believe while the preaching is in progress, but by the time Monday morning rolls around, you won't only *not* believe it, you won't even remember it."

"Try again, Stevie, I'll remember it."

"Yes," agreed Stephan, obviously warming to his subject. "That's only because you took it personally. I also took it personally, as did however many closet gays they had sitting in those pews. But you know what?"

"No, not really."

"Nobody, repeat *nobody* else took it personally. Or even believes it!"

"Oh, come on . . ."

"Okay, okay," shot back Stephan, rising to the challenge. "You didn't see him calling for volunteers for this army of his to fight us, did you? You didn't see him handing out assault rifles from the pulpit or calling for after-church target practice, did you? It was nothing but talk. A Sunday talk . . . not even a Sunday truth."

Frank propped up his chin with his thumb before verbally retaliating: "The first weapon of war is invariably propaganda. Before you're taught to use that assault rifle on your enemy, you're taught to *hate* that enemy." He threw up his hand like a traffic cop. "I suppose I could be wrong about Wheelwright. I suppose it's possible that he spoke out of ignorance instead of out of hatred. Maybe he could still be sympathetic."

"I really think so because he *is* a man of God, and

in the Bible doesn't it say that the Lord is full of compassion and mercy?"

Frank slid off the desk. "If you say so."

"Trust me on this, Frankie! If you knew your Bible you'd be much more upbeat. Jesus is our model and he walked and preached among the saints *and* the sinners alike." Both of Stephan's hands were now stretched out in a clearly pleading position. "And something else. Want me to tell you something funny?"

"Make me laugh!"

Stephan, who clearly was becoming wound up, seemed to take no notice of Frank's blatant skepticism. "All of these ministers who rail from their pulpit against us Sunday after Sunday are not just preaching hate; they're also preaching bad theology."

"How so?"

"Because they have scratched around and found some isolated verses from scripture, most with ambiguous meanings, taken out of context, that they use to justify hating homosexuals."

Frank feigned a yawn. "Yeah, but you still haven't made me laugh."

"Try to listen; this is important. The Ten Commandments do not mention homosexuality. And most significant, in all of Jesus' more than three thousand different teachings, there is not a word—not one single word—about homosexuality."

Frank's lips formed a tight, thin line. "I'm not one bit concerned about Jesus persecuting us. I'm concerned about Reverend Wheelwright and the Christian fundamentalists persecuting us."

Stephan waved a single index finger in the air. "Not so. Wheelwright, as a *Christian* minister, would have to be committed to Jesus' most important advice."

"And that is?"

"Jesus pleaded with his followers that if they forgot everything else he taught them there were two things they absolutely must never forget: to love the Lord thy God with all their hearts and all their might, and surely, Frankie, even you must know the second part."

"To love thy neighbor as thyself," Frank piped in, beaming proudly at his accomplishment.

"Precisely! Precisely!" Stephen applauded. "So now you can understand why Wheelwright has no choice. He must come to the aid of the victims, rather than the perpetrators."

Chapter 12

CARLA LIFTED THE lid of the cast-iron kettle and breathed deeply, savoring the aroma. To test the cubes of beef for tenderness, she poked them with a long-handled fork, and she estimated that it was the right time to throw in the potatoes and carrots. The zucchini could wait.

Almost by accident, she discovered nearly six years ago that she had something of a knack for cooking. That's when she wanted to buy her mother a cake *and* a present for her thirty-sixth birthday, but quickly discovered that she had money for one or the other but not both. Carla chose a pair of dangling earrings that moved through the air like miniature mobiles, and she made the birthday cake from scratch, a cherry angel-food cake that touched Judith so deeply that she had to use the sleeve of her blouse just to soak up the sudden rush of tears.

Carla heard the key turn in the lock and glanced up at the kitchen clock; surprisingly it was only a quarter after four. It was not at all like Judith to make it home until much before six or even six-thirty. The door opened and then quietly closed. In the front hall were the predictable sounds of envelopes ripping open. Not much mail today: a bill from the Rachetville Department of Water and Sewer, the magazine of the American Library Association, and a postcard from Aunt Marcia and Uncle Allan who were "having a wonderful time" in Delray Beach, Florida.

Heading toward the kitchen was the click-clack of high heels as they struck, perhaps harder than usual, against the polished hardwood floor. "Hello, love," the familiar voice sang out. "I'm home."

"In the kitchen, Mom."

Judith entered the furthermost room in the house, all the while untying the big red silk bow at her neck. "Hmmm," she stopped short, before lifting her head back to better take in the aromatic aroma. "Hungarian goulash. My favorite!"

"Uh, not quite, it's beef stew."

"Hmm, beef stew, my favorite."

Carla ground some fresh peppercorns into the simmering pot before turning to kiss her mother on the cheek. "Why do you suppose it is that I question your credibility?"

Judith shrugged. "Sure beats me."

"You know, you're home really early tonight? Dinner won't be ready for at least an hour."

"I had to get out of there! There was no way I could hang on until closing," she said, trying to stretch out the stress from the back of her head and neck. "Don't rush dinner. I'm going to sit in the tub for an hour, which should be enough time to wash the nonsense of the day from my body, if not from my spirit."

Carla replaced the heavy lid on the pot before more

carefully appraising her mother's condition. "Sounds ominous. What's up? I thought the burning issue over *Catcher in the Rye* and *The Grapes of Wrath* had now been settled."

Judith nodded. "Oh, that *has* been settled, albeit to nobody's satisfaction. Forty-seven books may not be displayed on the shelf, but they may be checked out *if* specifically requested. No, what's bothering me now is something else. And that happens to be the very latest, up-to-the-minute nonsense of the day!"

"Mom, how come so much happens to you? Makes me wonder if Mr. Peters, you know Karen Peters's daddy, has as much trouble running his big ol' Wal-Mart as you have running your little library?"

With something more than usual caution, Judith eyed her daughter for signs that she was about to become critical. Considering that this was one of her harshest days on the job ever, she knew that the last thing she needed was one more person pouring rubbing alcohol into her open wounds by telling her that she was not doing good work. Or, as in today's case, that she *was* doing "the devil's work." With slow and deliberate motions, Judith bent to pull off first one polished black pump and then the other before closing her eyes and pressing her back against the jamb of the kitchen door.

"Are you going to tell me?" Carla asked, her voice bright with unmet curiosity. "What happened?"

The librarian's eyes popped open and she found herself faintly smiling. It made her feel a bit better to realize that, yes, her daughter really was interested in her experiences. Also, she made a private note that she ought to be ashamed of herself for jumping to the terrible conclusion that her own flesh and blood was ready to pounce on her momentary weakness. "What happened to me was that I received an unexpected visit from the CCML."

"The what? Never heard of them."

"The Concerned Citizens for a Moral Library. It's a new organization whose mission is to purify libraries." Judith sighed as though she were growing too weak by the minute for much further discussion.

"And?"

"After an extremely unpleasant conversation, I asked them to leave."

"What do you think will happen?" Carla asked.

"I suppose they'll put pressure on the city fathers to get rid of me, and/or closely monitor me, waiting for me to trip up, anything that could help get me fired."

For a period of time, both women were quiet. Each needed something from the other but both needed a bit of time to figure out precisely what that need was. Judith realized that she needed a little tender loving concern. Why, for God's sake, should she be ashamed of it? After all, nobody gets too old or too independent for a little reassuring warmth from a loved one, do they?

"Mom," Carla said at last, "I know you've dedicated your life to standing up for the right thing. There's nothing wrong with that, but why, please tell me why, is it always *you*? Can't you give someone else a chance to play Joan of Arc for a change? If that's the way they want the library to be—well, they *do* represent the tax-payers, don't they? I mean, how much harm would it do if you'd swallow a little of your personal pride and do what everybody else does? For once in your life, couldn't you do what everybody else does? Just go along with the crowd?"

Chapter 13

JUST BEFORE THE supper hour on Thursday evening, Stephan drove the monster of a van into the practically empty parking lot of the Rachetville Baptist Church. Next to a late-model, black Lincoln Town Car with a clergy emblem bolted to its license plate, he cut the motor.

Nodding toward the oversized automobile, Frank asked, "Who was it that once said that man cannot serve both God and money, too?" Then shaking his head in obvious frustration over his inability to remember, he added mischievously, "Well, anyway, it's a fair assumption that that statement didn't originate with the Reverend Mr. Wheelwright."

As the men in lockstep walked toward the church's side entrance, Stephan turned his head toward his companion. "Trouble with you, Frank, is that you come from a long line of nonbelievers so you don't have experience dealing with men of God. Do us both a favor, and work at keeping your skepticism to yourself. Try being nice and charming and I promise you this: You're going to be in for a real surprise."

As soon as the secretary ushered the men into the small office with the large cross, the Reverend Roland Wheelwright, wearing a smile as wide as the whole out-of-doors, marched briskly around his desk and extended his outstretched hand. "Well, well, gentlemen, how nice to see you all. Please come on in and sit yourselves down, and tell me to what do I owe the pleasure of your company."

"It was certainly kind of you to see us at such short notice," said Stephan.

Frank added, "Yes, thank you, sir. We know how busy you must be; we appreciate it."

The preacher manufactured a series of little heh-heh-heh laughs. "I'm never too busy to take care of God's own people, no sir! I might also add that I'm not too busy to notice that you gentlemen never once returned to our church. Aren't you receiving our mailings? I distinctly remember taking your name and address, but I'm not certain if I gave it to Mrs. Mullens—she's the church secretary, and quite an efficient one at that. Been with this church for fifteen years—no, I take that back. I wouldn't want to lie!" He added a few more of his heh-heh-hehs.

"She's been with us almost two years longer than I've been the pastor of this church and I've already been here for fourteen years! My goodness! My goodness!" he said, shaking his head in mock disbelief. "How time does fly!"

"Uh, Reverend Wheelwright," Frank said, interrupting the minister's soliloquy. "We came here today to discuss an urgent matter which we believe you will be able to help us with."

"I trust you came to the right place because helping two such fine Christian gentlemen as yourselves would be a pleasure, truly a very great pleasure."

Stephan leaned forward in his armchair. "The reason we came to see you today is because we—Frank and I—are being constantly harassed by a member of your congregation." The thick, drooping lids of the preacher suddenly raised themselves.

"Somebody in my congregation? Are you sure? Why, who in my congregation would do such a terrible thing!?"

Frank peered directly into those freshly opened eyes before answering, "The teenage son of the owner of Harris's Hardware Store, Andy Harris."

The minister craned his neck forward. "You mean to tell me that Larry and Elna Harris's boy is playing little jokes on you men?"

"No, Reverend Wheelwright," replied Frank sharply. "Not at all *little* jokes. He has written letters," he explained, holding toward the preacher a packet of crinkly blue-gray envelopes. On the upper left-hand corner of each envelope were the oversized letters A.H., RACHETVILLE, ARKANSAS. "All fifteen of these letters are signed 'Avenging Hero.' We've received dozens of obscene and threatening phone calls. They—"

"Gentlemen! Gentlemen!" he intoned. "Come now! Let's reason together. You say these letters are signed 'Avenging Hero' but not actually 'Andy Harris.' You're receiving *incoming* telephone calls and since you did not actually *see* the actual faces of the callers, I can almost guarantee that this is nothing more than a rather unfortunate case of mistaken identity."

"Reverend Wheelwright!" cried out both Frank and Stephan at more or less the same moment.

Reverend Wheelwright raised his hands as though he were stopping traffic. "Please . . . please give me the courtesy of allowing me to explain exactly why I said what I did. First of all, I have personally known and admired the Harrises ever since I've been here at Rachetville Baptist—fourteen years. They're fine, fine people, religious people! And as far as their son—well, Andy is a good boy. Neat as a pin and just as religious as they come. If only all young men were like Andy Harris, it would be a different world. I guarantee you that; it would be a *very* different world, indeed!"

"Mr. Wheelwright, I can understand and even appreciate your natural reluctance to believe something bad about someone you like," explained Frank. "But let me say that there is no question, absolutely no question whatsoever, about Andy Harris's involvement. He with two of his friends, Douglas Crawford and Michael Horten, smashed a steaming pizza in Stephan's face, causing him to suffer very painful first-degree burns. The harassment has gotten worse and continues to this day."

This time the clergyman seemed to sit up a little straighter to stare unblinkingly at Stephan. "You don't mean to say that *our* Andy Harris did that to you!?"

"Yes, Reverend Wheelwright," Stephan answered returning his gaze. "That's *exactly* what he did to me. Why else would we be here?"

The aging man ran his fingers through his fine crop of gray hair. "Hard to believe that boy would do something like that. I can tell you one thing, he's certainly carrying his fun and games far too far."

Both Frank and Stephan allowed themselves the

bare beginnings of a smile, but it was Stephan who spoke. "So do you think you could help us . . . put a stop to this?"

The minister offered a rapid-fire response. "Consider it done!"

A deep sigh of relief was audibly heard coming from either Frank or Stephan, or maybe both, but it was Frank who picked up and carefully nurtured the conversational ball. "What, if I may ask, do you intend to do?"

Mr. Wheelwright looked up from the heavy gold insignia ring he had been turning round and round on a pudgy fourth finger where there was a virtual garden of coarse, black hair. "Naturally, I'll phone the boy, ask him to come in for a little chat. Then I'll ask him to confess his transgressions before his pastor . . . and his Lord. Finally I'll make him repent those sins before his pastor . . . and his Lord, making him promise to behave himself."

Stephan shot an I-told-you-so look in Frank's direction before rising to his feet. He rebuttoned the middle button of his blue blazer before reaching out to share a final farewell shake with his host. "I really appreciate your willingness to help us, Reverend Wheelwright, and I hope that some day soon I'll be able to do something for you. All you have to do is ask."

As the minister escorted the men out of his office into the large adjoining social hall, he said, "I'm going to take you up on your offer to return my favor, Mr. Jones, and sooner than you think."

Frank interjected. "I assure you, that's okay with us, and that the offer my partner made holds equally true for me, too."

"Wonderful!" exulted Mr. Wheelwright while heartily patting both men on their backs. "Wonderful! But first let me clear up the little misunderstanding that has developed between you and the Harris boy and then I'm going to take you up on the favor that you offered. I'm going to ask you both to join our church and to become just two more people who are God's people."

Stephan threw Frank a pleading look, and then Frank shrugged mightily before answering. "Well . . . I guess—oh, sure, why not?"

The delighted preacher slapped their backs and squeezed their arms while exclaiming, "That's wonderful, really wonderful, and I'm truly gratified that two fine Christian gentlemen such as yourselves will join our fellowship." He then rubbed the top of his full head of steel-gray hair as a puzzled look crept across his face. "There is one thing, though, that for the life of me I just can't figure out."

Stephan, who by now had his arm draped around the preacher's shoulder, asked, "And what is that, Reverend Wheelwright?"

"Two such fine men as you. . . ." The minister shook his head in disbelief. "Well, for the life of me, I just can't understand what Andy Harris, or anybody else, could possibly find about you two Christian gentlemen to dislike."

The quiet became deafening. What normally could not be heard at all was now heard with excruciating volume: three men breathing in and breathing out; the rattle of an aging pickup truck a block and a half away on lower Prescott Avenue; even the sounds of Mrs. Mullens's ballpoint pen as it rolled effortlessly across the cash receivable book.

Frank swallowed back a sudden excess of saliva. "You mean . . . you really don't know?"

Mr. Wheelwright's face was a study in innocence. "Know? Know what?"

"What Frank is trying to tell you," choked Stephan, while self-consciously dropping his arm from the preacher's shoulder, "is that Frank and I are . . . are a couple."

The minister's bushy eyebrows skipped halfway up his forehead. "You don't mean to stand there and tell me that you two . . . two Christian gentlemen . . ." He paused as though he didn't know what to say next, or maybe it was only that he paused because he was too stunned to say what he *thought* ought to come next.

Stephan thrust his hands, palms up, mere inches above the clergyman's abundant waist. A casual observer might come to the quick, but terribly wrong, conclusion that a surprisingly well dressed beggar was pleading for a little bread, instead of the absolutely correct conclusion that a young man was fervently begging for a few crumbs of understanding. "What we want you to understand, Reverend Wheelwright, is that come August fifteenth, Frank and I will have been together for five years. Hey, I bet that's longer than some of those marriages that you officiate at in your beautiful sanctuary."

Suddenly, the minister's cheeks puffed and his face reddened as though his internal temperature was rapidly heating up to a combustibly high level. "You *dare* to compare the sanctified love of a man and a woman with the sodomy of two men? That's blasphemy! Blasphemy, I tell you!" The preacher shouted. With his hamlike hands he grasped each man's head, knocking the men off balance and sending them to their knees.

"Dost thou," he cried, his eyes staring wildly at the

ceiling of the Rachetville Baptist Church's social hall. "Dost thou renounce the devil and all his works, the vain pomp and glory of the world, with all covetous desires of the same, and the sinful desires of the flesh, so that thou will not follow, nor be led by them?"

"What *are* you doing?" Frank asked as first he and then Stephan stumbled to their feet.

The preacher's forehead exuded sweat, cold sweat. "Can't you see? Can't you tell? I'm washing you in the cleansing blood of Jesus Christ Our Savior! I'm giving you Holy Baptism so that you both may be born again!"

Frank vigorously shook his head. "But we're not here for that, not here for salvation!"

"Then what!?" asked the clergyman, allowing his veiled eyelids to again raise themselves, only this time maybe even higher than they had ever been raised before.

Stephan sighed wearily and audibly before attempting his answer. "For one of the most precious things that any human being could ever ask of another: compassion."

"*Compassion!*" shrieked the minister, his complexion now taking on a bluish-purplish hue. "There is *no* compassion for sodomites! And there certainly is *no* compassion for those who commit the worst sin of them all. Read your Bible, because there it is written that the one sin that can never be forgiven is the sin of blasphemy."

"Blasphemy, is it?" taunted Frank. "You would really call it blasphemy because Stephan makes the undeniably true observation that not all marriages entered into at this church of yours have lasted as long as our relationship? Well, *Reverend,* it so happens that I may not have read the Bible, but I have read my history and that's why I can tell you this: If Stephan is guilty of blasphemy, why then, he's in damn good company because both the Bible and history teach of two men who have been tried, convicted, and finally put to death for the crime of blasphemy. Maybe you know them? Their names were Socrates and Jesus Christ."

Chapter 14

WITH A PRACTICED hand, Carla brushed her auburn hair, which shone with an inbred luster reserved for the young, the healthy, and the beautiful. By the time she had slipped the saffron party dress over her head, she looked as though there were nothing she could possibly add or subtract that would make her look more radiantly beautiful than she looked right at this moment.

And as she inserted a pearl earring into her lobe, she became aware that Judith was standing at the threshold of her room. "You know, you were right, Mom," she said with a quick toss of her head. "The pearls really do work better than the rhinestones."

Judith smiled because she found her daughter's words resonating through her: ... *you were right, Mom*. She *really* liked savoring the moment while trying to remember exactly how long it had been since she had heard her daughter speak those words. Not for quite a while. For way too long a while.

However, there used to be a time, and not all that long ago, when Judith would come home brimming with her stories of the never-ending struggle at the library against too many demands on too few resources. Even when she was able to foster an uneasy peace on that front, there was always the second front to contend with! That was the force that was inevitably led by a sincere and vocal group who fought tirelessly for what they believed. What they believed was that it was the duty of the library to reflect only the values that were *their* values. After all, weren't they the ones, the only ones, with a personal relationship to Christ Jesus?

Judith often found comfort in telling *real* behind-the-scenes stories to Carla because her daughter was absolutely therapeutic when she'd cheer her mother's victories and rail against her defeats.

But ever since Andy Harris had charged into Carla's life, Judith noticed that the only time she seemed to gain her daughter's complete approval was when she waved high her personal white flag of compromise or defeat.

Although Judith's last tension-filled conflict had taken place a few weeks earlier, she was too afraid of Carla's recent lack of empathy for her feelings to even mention it. It started innocently enough when the library in celebration of Earth Day put up a display titled, "In the Beginning . . ." On the display table were a collection of books by renowned physicists, geologists, social anthropologists, archaeologists, and others giving their most current and reasoned explanation of how life evolved on this planet. The paint wasn't yet dry on the poster-board sign when Mrs. Wooten stormed in demanding that the "unholy" display be taken down and the books returned to the back library stacks "where they'd do less harm." Mrs. Wooten's problem was that these "tainted" books were at odds with the two-thousand-year-old explanation that had already been offered in Genesis.

When Judith had refused to either take down the sign or break up the display, Hilda Wooten temporarily retreated to the comfort of her long and luxurious ranch-style home to dial a few choice phone numbers from her well-turned Rolodex. Before the day was over, Judith was paid an unexpected visit by Mr. Randall McDowell, the chairman of the library's board of trustees. His straight-to-the-point ultimatum was delivered in agonizingly plain view and clear hearing of the library's staff.

What he said was, "*You* go or *it* goes! It's one or the other!" Mr. McDowell threatened, shaking his stern index finger at a humiliated and speechless librarian. "Can't you get it in your head, can't you finally understand, Mrs. Wayland, that this is a God-fearing community that doesn't want to read anything that will dilute their faith!?"

At that moment, Judith was convinced that she could physically feel each and every one of those dozen or so pairs of eyes devouring her *and* her privacy. She made it a point—perhaps a small, but still and all, a very important point—to lift her chin before walking erect, without a word, back to her own private office and quietly closing the door.

As Judith entered her book-lined office with its drab mustard-and-black floor tiles, she was struck by one fact, the one and only thing at that moment she was completely certain of. The simple fact was that by the time she left her room, she'd be different. Changed forever by the decision that she had had thrust upon her. But how could she live with herself if she scuttled science and learning in favor of religion and superstition? Then again, how could she live at all if she didn't? Because who would hire a forty-two-year-old head librarian who had been fired by the Rachetville Library's board of trustees for insubordination? Particularly at a time when library jobs were being cut everywhere.

Fifteen minutes later, Judith marched out of her office straight to the front of the building where the display books were now being examined with consummate interest by a twelve- or thirteen-year-old boy. She reached up to remove the offending poster-board sign and saw that her hands had begun to tremble.

Although this incident had happened a few weeks ago, Judith still had not found the "right" time to speak to Carla about her situation. What she needed was for the one person she loved more than anyone else to share her pain at her loss of autonomy as well as her constantly mourned loss of integrity. Even though she had hated the bargain she had struck, taking the sign down but not getting rid of the books, she wondered if she wouldn't have hated even more losing her livelihood precisely five days before her mortgage payment was due?

Maybe, she reasoned, if Carla could understand exactly why she had done what she did and forgive her, then maybe she could learn to forgive herself.

Judith fastened the clasp of Carla's pearl necklace. "You look lovely," she whispered while her whole being resonated with pride as well as with thoughts of the long-gone Roy Wayland. Did he, she wondered, at least from time to time, have any conception of what he was missing? What pleasures could he have possibly found amid uncaring strangers that could conceivably compare with the joy of seeing your own child turn into a woman, a woman both lovely and loving?

"Tell me," Judith asked with a smile, "are you really that same little person who I used to play with in your sandpile, building sand castles not so very many years ago?"

Carla twirled around to give her mother a hug of such intensity that Judith understood at once that some special feelings were being unleashed. Finally in a voice raw with emotion, the girl whispered, "Thank you."

"For what?" Judith asked, as much surprised as she was overwhelmed.

Carla shook her head as though she were at a loss to commit such a surge of feelings to the scrutiny of words. But finally she took a stab, "I don't know. . . for this dress—so much expense just so I'd look nice for the prom. And also for that compliment. I guess I needed that."

"You *needed* that?" Judith looked taken aback. "I thought you've been sitting on top of the world ever since Andy started dating you regularly and invited you to be his prom date!"

"Well . . . I am. Only I wouldn't want him to have second thoughts or anything now that he's stuck with me."

"Oh, really!" interjected Judith, impatient with her overripened sense of humility or lack of self-esteem. "Why do you have to be constantly reminded that you're bright and pretty—and, if I may add, a hell of a lot more mature than your rabidly homophobic boyfriend?"

"Oh, no, Mom, Andy's not like that anymore! Nowadays he leaves those guys strictly alone. You know, I really think he's a lot more grown up than he used to be."

"Hmmm," murmured Judith, looking a long way from being convinced.

"Yes, he really is! He's stopped bothering them. Doesn't that prove something?"

"Well, it might prove it somewhat more convincingly if I hadn't noticed that there are more floodlights focused on the Forgotten Treasures Antique Shop than on the Parson Springs Savings Bank."

"Can't you for once ever give him the benefit of the doubt?" Carla implored. "Andy hasn't done any pranks for weeks and weeks, and I know *that* for a fact."

This time it was Judith who looked perplexed. "But I thought they—didn't you tell me that Andy was warned that their phones were tapped?"

Carla went back to carefully following the line of her lips with the lipstick brush. "I really think that knowing that merely gave him the excuse to stop doing what he was already feeling pretty ashamed of doing. I doubt they really had their phone tapped anyway."

At seven-thirty, the doorbell at the Wayland home chimed. Carla and Judith spontaneously turned to look at each other as though neither had a clear idea what to do next. "I'll let him in," Judith offered.

As she swung open the front door, Judith was, in spite of herself, taken aback with how handsomely resplendent Andy looked. Standing in his white dinner jacket with the scarlet cummerbund, he seemed like a young and valiant prince, and she saw how her daughter could find his looks so appealing. She felt strangely stupid having to fight off feelings of insecurity. Why hadn't she thought to put on fresh makeup, or at the very least, to comb her hair?

Self-consciously, Judith tucked her blouse inside her skirt as she glanced around the living room. When had the furniture become so old and worn? Pointing toward an oversized chair with a flowered chintz slipcover, she beckoned to him to sit down. "Oh, please come on in, Andy. Carla will be ready in a minute."

"Oh, here," he said, offering Judith an orchid inside a see-through box. "Probably she'll want to pin it on her dress."

"Yes, I'm sure she will," she agreed, returning with it to Carla's bedroom.

When Judith returned to the living room, she looked prettier, after the quick addition of a little powder and paint. She smiled, wondering what she could say to make him feel comfortable. "Congratulations, Andy, on being accepted to Duke University. That's a fine school!"

Andy nodded, showing his pleasure that Judith was aware of his accomplishment. "My dad wants me to get a degree in business administration, but . . . I'm not sure. . . ."

Judith looked interested, and that in itself was encouragement enough to spur him on. "Dad thinks that the opportunities for business right here in Atkins County are nothing short of miraculous!" He laughed. "If it were up to him, he'd already have calling cards printed saying Lawrence Harris and Son."

"Well, whatever you do, don't knock being in business for yourself." She thought of her own fears of being fired, which she controlled so nicely during her waking and working hours. But at night—ah, the nights, now wasn't that a very different story?

A minute later Carla swept into the room. Andy smiled with such sweet yet shy appreciation that Judith felt ashamed for so long being critical of the boy. A few sentences passed back and forth between the couple—how pretty the orchid was, how crowded the backseat would be because of Doug and Donna, Mike and Lisa. It wasn't the words, but the timid smiles and gracious glances they exchanged that spoke far more meaningfully than their ordinary, everyday words.

"Well," said Judith, opening the door for the departing couple, "I'd say have fun, but I can tell that it's completely unnecessary." Carla gave her mother a sudden embrace and then they were gone, heading toward the Harrises' Oldsmobile waiting at the curb.

Chapter 15

FRANK BACKED THE monster out of the garage and around to the front of the house. He craned his neck for Stephan, who should have been hurrying out the front door to meet him. But no such luck. Why was it, he wondered, when Stephan said he was ready, and when he *looked* as though he were ready, still and all, he wasn't ready.

If tardiness showed a lack of respect for other people's time, then shouldn't he give Stephan a good piece of his mind? With his fist, he struck the vehicle's horn. He felt his annoyance building. It wasn't even the three, five, or even ten minutes that he would be waiting that made him so mad. What was really steaming him up was the fear that Stephan didn't care enough about him to be on time.

Frank closed his eyes and dropped his head against the steering wheel. The argument, if they had one, would revolve around Frank's demand that his partner arrive at a destination precisely when he was expected. Undoubtedly that's what they would argue about. But deep down Frank knew that was not the real concern. Frank couldn't help that clumsily knotted up inside of him was the feeling that: Frank Feels Angry Because He Doesn't Feel Loved Enough.

But this night was meant for celebrating, not for bickering. Today they would mark the ten-month anniversary of their time in Parson Springs. Business was good, better even than they had dared hope. They were beginning to make a friend or two, and even that trouble early on with those three boys seemed to be a thing of the past—albeit the not-yet-forgotten past.

During those weeks of intense harassment, Frank had felt as though he were suffering from a dull but relentless headache. An early-to-bed, early-to-rise headache from which he would never break free. It seemed so insoluble at the time. No one exactly rushed to their aid. But eventually it was resolved. Two dawn-to-dusk floodlights outside their store and a tap on their phone made Andy Harris back off. Frank wondered if the kid had gotten bored with writing letters without receiving any response. He didn't really care. It was over and done with and that was relief enough.

The door of the recreational vehicle swung open and Stephan hopped in. As he slid into the passenger's seat, Frank sniffed the air. "Hey, that's my cologne you're wearing!"

Stephan wrinkled his nose. "Don't you just love it?"

At the Blue Spruce Inn they were seated at a candlelit table overlooking foggy Baxter Pond where they toasted Forgotten Treasures. After feasting on crispy duck in orange sauce, they had a second round of toasts. The dessert, lemon cheesecake with raspberry sauce, was so good that it inspired still another round of toasts.

By nine o'clock their dessert plates had been cleared, their wine bottle had been drained, and yet there was still too much life in the ol' night to call it a night.

"How about going to the bar at the top of the hotel?" suggested Stephan. "We could listen to some country and western music?"

As the two men strolled through the ornate, turn-of-the-century lobby of the Majestic Hotel, which sat serenely on top of the uppermost crest of Magic Mountain, they were drawn to the sounds of live music coming from the softly lit ballroom.

On the opposite side of the dance floor, a divinely happy Carla and Andy were dancing. She was thrilled beyond belief that the once-elusive Andy Harris was not only her prom date, but her very attentive boyfriend. She pressed herself still closer, which suddenly alarmed him. "Hey, don't go getting lipstick on my jacket!" he warned. "If my daddy doesn't get his fifty-buck deposit back on this tux, he'll kill me. Honest-to-God, he will!"

Taking a look inside the festive ballroom, Frank and Stephan observed a sea of young men in rented tuxedos and an even larger sea of young men who evidently didn't have the price of a rented tux. These were the ones wearing their Sunday-best blue suits. But with or without tux, each held a girl in her best frilly finery in his arms. Watching that, Stephan turned away in sadness and in anger. "My God, I wish I could shake those dancers—try to make them understand how lucky they are."

Frank did a double take. "How so?"

"You know, they can't *possibly* appreciate how privileged they are. How could they?" Stephan tossed his head back toward the ballroom. "They're free! They have *always* been free because they've never had to hide their feelings. For them it's okay not only to feel love, but also to show it."

Concerned, Frank beckoned Stephan to follow. They entered a deserted function room petitioned off from the main ballroom by only a mustard-colored accordion room divider. From the other side, the band began playing a modern love song about being lost, lonely, and afraid, "Until Love Came My Way." Stephan knew the lyrics and his eyes seemed connected with Frank's as he sang with a voice ripe with feeling. A voice that could have told the composer-lyricist a thing or two or three about being alone and lonely "Until Love Came My Way. . . ."

AS THE HOURS flew by and the prom progressed, the music and the dancing grew increasingly loud and animated.

When a song ended, the shaggy-haired leader of the combo stepped up to the standing mike and raised his hands. "It's now five minutes before midnight, so the next number will be the last dance, and . . ."

The spontaneous groans of the revelers drowned out his next words. The musician whistled loudly into the microphone, and that went a long way toward settling everyone down. "Thanks a bunch you all for inviting yours truly, Dave and his Wildmen, to entertain you at your senior prom. We hope you'll have us play for you again sometime real soon. We're going to end with a great treat. The girl voted "Most Talented" member of the senior class, Sherry Ingalls, has agreed to sing the last song of the night. Please give a big hand to Sherry singing, 'My Great Love.' "

Andy's arms slid around Carla's waist as he whispered softly into her ear, "Found you!" She smiled and whispered, "You know you never lost me."

Prancing up from amid the wildly enthusiastic crowd to the stage, slender Sherry Ingalls began singing in her reedy voice, "I found my love . . . my own great love tucked in your arms."

Andy enveloped Carla in his arms. And if there were some sort of scale that could measure human happiness, just one passing glance would reveal that here at last was one couple whose reading would be high, very, very high.

Minutes later amid waves, raucous cheers, and elaborate farewells, the three couples who had come to the party together left laughing together through the dignified marble and mahogany lobby. By the time they reached the rear parking lot, there was already a long procession of cars queuing up for a more-or-less orderly exit.

Donna moaned as did her date, Doug the Ironman. "Oh, no, we'll never get out of here!" he added.

"Don't worry 'cause that won't matter when you see what I've got," exclaimed Andy as he pulled Carla into his trot. "One look and you won't care how long it takes us to leave." Obediently the others loped along behind them until reaching the rear of the Olds. Andy inserted his key into the trunk lock. "Come feast your eyes." As the trunk opened the light went on and an oversized red cooler was exposed. And everyone saw it was filled to capacity with ice and frosty cans of beer. Andy beamed. "A graduation gift from my old man."

Chapter 16

Aт Skipper's Bar on the penthouse floor of the grand old hotel, Frank and Stephan sat at a table next to a wall of glass. It was nearly one o'clock in the morning, and the music played by Jerry at the piano had become mellower. "If a genie popped out to grant me three wishes," said Frank, "I'd probably waste one wishing that the Red Sox would win the world series. I know they never will. I swear they've got a death wish."

"Does your Red Sox wish come before or *after* your wish for a vehicle that doesn't require three parking places? One wish of mine," continued Stephan, "is being at an art auction and the only one to recognize that the painting coming up on the block was by an Old Master. My favorite fantasy, though, is becoming a great stand-up comic."

Frank registered mild surprise. "Are you serious? I've never heard you tell a joke."

"That's only because I'm not a great stand-up comic."

Frank laughed and then from the laughter, his face took on a more thoughtful look. "What if," he asked, striking his own chest with his index finger, "I had the power to grant one and only one wish for you. What would your most cherished wish be?"

"Are you getting tired? I am."

"Why you faker! You don't want to tell me, do you?"

"Maybe . . . another time."

Frank gazed out the window and realized that this less than a speck on the map of Arkansas had captured his love. This crazy town *and* Stephan Jones.

"All right," relented Stephan. "I'll tell you, but consider yourself warned."

"So considered."

"I'd like us to become active members—firm believers in a church, one that preaches love and yet doesn't stray too far from a strict, literal interpretation of the Bible."

"Ohh, I was hoping you'd request something easy like a ride on the next space shuttle. Look, I don't have any objection to sometimes attending church with you, most any church, but . . ."

"But?"

Frank's next words came with a rush. "How can you expect me to turn into a Bible-thumping, foot-stomping convert when I actually believe that some of their teachings are misguided?"

Stephan looked as though he were edging toward exasperation. "You think I like the way they rant and rage against us gays? You *actually* think I like it any more than you do? To us, homophobia may be *everything,* but it's not everything! Besides, the churches are changing, Frank; wake up and smell the coffee. My God, the ministry attracts gays like hairstyling or interior design."

Frank grinned mischievously. "Or antiques?"

"So the more gay people who enter the ministry ... and the more of us that attend these churches, well, the faster you're going to see these needed changes happen."

"Let's be optimistic and say you're right and that this more compassionate response eventually comes to pass. It's still, as you've so correctly pointed out, not everything. It doesn't even come close."

Stephan shrugged. "Don't let me stop you."

"Okay, laying aside fundamental churches' traditional hostility toward gays, I believe the way they view children is equally harmful."

Stephan shook his head vigorously. "Oh, come on, Frank. These churches love children. They're concerned with the entire family structure; even you ought to know that!"

"Hear me out, and then answer this question yes or no."

"Shoot!"

"When you read what leading educators, psychiatrists, and well-known pediatricians advise us about raising children, at least on one issue they all seem to speak with a single voice—they all urge us to nurture children's self-esteem."

"No informed opinion would disagree with that advice, but exactly what's your point, Frankie?"

"My point is obvious. All experts' advice flies directly in the face of what these churches are preaching. Christian doctrine preaches that babies who are as innocent as freshly laid eggs are 'born in original sin.' "

Frank struck the table with his fist. "Born in original sin! And you really believe that dogma like that is going to nurture self-esteem?"

"Well," said Stephan, rubbing his pale-as-porcelain forehead. "What the experts say doesn't necessarily mean that it's the church position that's wrong."

Frank flashed a victory grin. "True, but it doesn't necessarily mean that it's the church position that is correct, either."

This time it was Stephan who turned his head to gaze thoughtfully through the glass wall up and out to the heavens above, where the moon now seemed to be playing peek-a-boo behind the ever-thickening clouds.

Reaching across the table, Frank lightly touched the back of his partner's hand. "If I offended you, I'm sorry. Faith can give comfort and I'd never want to take that away from you. So, if you want me to attend church with you—any church, then just say the word."

"You still don't understand, do you?" Stephan's voice was low and urgent at the same time. "I want you to do a hell of a lot more than attend church with me. I pray every day that you'll come to accept Jesus Christ as your Lord and Savior and be born again! Don't you see? Can't you understand? I gave up theological school but I've never ever given up my faith. What I'm trying to tell you is that I must be with you. Both in this life and in the life to come."

Chapter 17

As FRANK AND Stephan strolled across the hotel's front parking lot, the moon slipped out of hiding long enough to illuminate the monster resting in a pool of gasoline. This was the result, they wearily realized, of the van having hit that bone-jarring hole in the road on the way to the Majestic. Happily, the RV started easily and drove well, even though there was a ruptured gas tank. Unhappily, however, the gas tank was quickly emptying out.

By the time they reached the bottom of the mountain road where it fed onto Route 62, the men decided to bypass home and go straight to Campbell Yaw's auto repair shop. They wouldn't be open at this time of the night, but at least the monster wouldn't have to be towed.

"Now," Frank observed, "if only the fuel holds out until we reach Yaw's."

As the wounded RV rolled west on Route 62 toward Ratchetville, there was almost no road traffic, although the motels still had their vacancy signs lit. There'd be pretty poor pickings tonight.

"Cam Yaw's place can't be much farther," explained Stephan, who was behind the wheel, to a surprisingly placid Frank. "Maybe a mile. Not much more than a mile."

Frank craned his neck, checking the fuel gauge for any sign of movement. Silently and anxiously they watched the distance decrease while the gas decreased, praying that the distance would disappear sometime before the gas did. This time around, luck was with them. Over on the right, not two hundred yards past the Tastee-Freeze stand, was the sign that they were waiting for: THE CAMPBELL S. YAW AUTO SERVICE CENTER. Although the sign was lighted, the free-standing cinder-block building was blacker than a witch's heart.

Stephan successfully steered the gleaming hulk onto the paved front yard of the building before allowing himself one mighty sigh of relief, and finally turned off the motor. Had this been any night besides Saturday, they might have made themselves comfortable in the RV until morning, when Cam could have driven them home. Problem was, like most local businesses, Cam Yaw's place was closed on Sunday, that being the Lord's day.

As the men walked along the dark and nearly deserted strip of highway, Stephan pointed to a sign at the side of the road: RACHETVILLE 4. "Hey, it's not so bad! That means we're only three miles from Parson Springs."

Frank rubbed his eyes. "Yeah, well, I don't feel like walking three more miles."

"Considering how late it is now and how early we got up, I'm surprised you even feel like breathing."

The night was warm, the moon was full for the moment, and from the lush and luxuriant forest of the Ozarks there came a range of summer sounds: a convention of crickets, a screech owl, and at least one desperately-lonely-for-love coyote.

When the men reached the bridge over the Pascaloosa, Stephan stopped short, putting his hand to his ear. "Listen, something's heading this way. Maybe a truck."

Moments later, one of the Tyson's Chicken Company's sixteen-wheelers, loaded with stack upon stack of plastic poultry crates filled to cramped capacity with chickens, came barreling down the highway. Frank wildly waved his hands and shouted as though he were trying to attract the attention of the Almighty: "Taxi! Taxi! Hey, taxi!!!"

The grizzly faced driver, who up to this moment thought he had seen *everything,* did a double take, his jaw drooped, and he shook his head in wonderment. Apparently, being mistaken for a cab was beyond his previous bag of experiences. At least up until now it had been.

"Taxi?" asked a perplexed Stephan as the great truck went highballing down the road. "What the hell did you yell 'taxi' for?"

Frank slipped off his linen jacket and leaned against the bridge's iron guardrail. " 'Cause I couldn't, on the spur of the moment, come up with any other single word meaning 'Drive us home. We'll pay the fare.' "

Leaning against the bridge's rusty and crusty rail, the men gazed in quiet admiration at the serpentine turns of the swollen river below. "What a racket water makes!"

Pointing downstream, Stephan exclaimed, "Well, no wonder! Can you see them? Look at those rapids!"

Because of the river's crashing, splashing noises, neither Stephan nor Frank was aware of the hum of the heavy car's motor until it was almost upon them. At the last possible moment, Frank jumped quickly into the road and thrust his right thumb high into the air. "Can't you see they're going the other way," called out Stephan, still mesmerized by the primordial call of the swiftly moving waters below.

The black power-car zoomed over the bridge on its way back to Rachetville, its six young occupants at first far too involved with their own lives to take much notice or interest in a couple of poor, unfortunate hitchhikers. But after he'd driven some ways down the road Andy suddenly slammed on the brakes. "Dear Jesus!" he yelped. "It's them! It's the fags!" And in an unexpected and flashy maneuver he spun the car around in such a way that it looked as if he were a contestant in the Indianapolis 500.

If Andy's obsession with the men had been dormant, it certainly wasn't dead. Pressing the accelerator flat against the floorboard, he exclaimed, "It's them! Sweet Jesus! I *know* it's them!"

Carla reluctantly raised her resting head from the shoulder of her man. She had been feeling gloriously excited by the unaccustomed alcohol that had raced through all the main routes and byways of her now-supercharged bloodstream. No doubt that she felt somehow different than she had ever felt before because she had drunk more than she had ever drunk before. Two beers, *only* two beers may not sound like a lot, but for a novice drinker, it was more than enough.

She felt so-o-o good. She thought it funny that she had never before noticed how wonderfully perfect this old world really was. Andy, of course, was perfect, but so was everybody in the car. Absolutely perfect! And surprise of all surprises, for the first time in her life, she, Carla Abigail Wayland, was perfectly perfect too!

Even the speeding Oldsmobile added to the high excitement that had not only invaded her senses, but conquered them. She felt so very special that she was convinced that if she really wanted to, she could reach out and hug the whole world. She possessed power enough to make certain that Andy Harris would never stop loving her and that nothing bad could ever again touch her. "Well, what are you going to do, Andy?" she asked, feeling an unexplained attack of the giggles coming on. But the narrowly focused look he wore of pure, dead-on concentration excluded answering anybody, anybody at all.

"All right, then, have it your way!" she announced good-naturedly. She began rhythmically singing and clapping, "Go Andy Go!" Laughing and teasing, Donna and Lisa followed by Spider and the Ironman joined in. "Go Andy Go!" Now they were all together and all really belting it out. "Ohh, Go Andy Go!!! Go Andy Go! Go! Go!! Go!!"

The car sped back down the highway, its high beams punching bright, shining holes through the darkness. Not more than a few hundred feet from where the men were originally sighted, those beams picked up the sight of them. With suit jackets slung jauntily over their shoulders, they were leisurely strolling across the Pascaloosa Bridge back toward Parson Springs. And as they walked, Stephan was singing, "I must be who I am . . . take me or leave me . . . only let me be free . . . free to be who I am . . ."

Andy dead-aimed his car straight at the two blissfully unaware walkers. Both Carla and the Ironman stared with a growing sense of frozen disbelief before finally screaming: "*Brake! Brake!!*" At the last moment possible, Andy slammed his foot against the brake, making the car veer crazily to the right before finally screeching and grinding to an ear-piercing halt.

As a stunned Frank absorbed the situation he was surprised to hear bombarding inside his head words from his old college ROTC instructor: To defeat the enemy, divide the enemy.

Violently he shoved a nearly paralyzed Stephan forward, broke into a run, and shouted, "Run, Steve! RUN!" Frank raced off in the opposite direction from Stephan, who finally began racing back across the bridge.

The door on the driver's side swung open and Andy lunged. It was this last, crazed action that careened into Carla's bubble of enchantment and shattered the spell.

Carla tried to grab hold of Andy's wrist while crying out, "What *are* you doing!?" She felt swept by shame that moments earlier she had egged him on with her raucous cheers.

Catching only a scraping of his fine, young skin beneath her polished pink nails, she watched in stricken silence as Andy, quickly followed by Spider, Ironman, and even the high-heeled Donna and Lisa, piled out of the car to race with a kind of frenzied fever after their all-too-human prey.

Although Frank Montgomery raced across the bridge as though his life depended upon it, Andy Harris was clearly narrowing the gap. Less than twenty feet separated him from his intended victim when Andy turned his head to glance behind, but nobody was there backing him up. Not Ironman, not even Spider. At that moment, Andy seemed to lose all interest in the chase.

Carla, looking and acting as though she had just undergone electroshock therapy, finally stumbled out of the car. Standing alone in the middle of the bridge, she heard the harsh panting, raspy puffing, and occasional bursts of profanity coming now from the combatants somewhere at the far edge of the bridge.

Suddenly she slapped a hand across her mouth. Although she felt like vomiting, she also felt like screaming, but she didn't do either. For an instant she wondered if she was still too much her mother's daughter to be like everyone else and to enjoy fun and games like the others. Or could it possibly be that the problem was that Andy and the others didn't have enough compassion to understand when something is anything but fun and games?

Then she was aware of how the sounds had changed. She heard the crash of racing feet. The chase was taking place down below, somewhere down on the river's dry and leafy shore. Carla could hear the swishing, swaying, and cracking of branches as well as the thud of footsteps landing hard in quick succession on dry and rotting branches. But most disturbing of all, she heard the curses and groans of various contenders straining desperately to either hide or to seek.

"AHHHHHHHHhhhhhh!!!!" The cry splintered the night and sent chills of foreboding streaking up Carla's spinal column.

"I *got* me one!" shrilled Spider. "I caught me a fucking faggot!" A jubilant Andy whooped and hollered back his congratulations along with his order to escort the prisoner back onto the bridge. "Hey, which one did you catch!?"

"The little fairy and our old pal Stephanie!"

Less than five minutes later, the celebrating Spider and Ironman marched Stephan Jones—head bowed, hands held behind his back—back to where Andy waited with sweet although barely contained anticipation. Although Spider may have made the capture, and Ironman may have secured the prisoner, there was no question who was running the show. With legs spread apart in the supradominant male stance, Andy began barking out orders as though he had been born taking private lessons from the cream of the Gestapo's high command.

Cupping his hands, he yelled directly into the right ear of the prisoner. "Drop to your knees, faggot! You fucking Stephanie Jones, son of a whore, son of a bitch, Goddamn queer bastard!"

Stephan's mouth was a thin, pink line. His eyes were clenched tightly shut, as though by shutting out the view, he could somehow shut out the physical pain ricocheting around his auditory canal, which felt like it was being attacked by a platoon of straight pins. Although his lips were ever-so-slightly moving, it was impossible to hear Stephan's words over a combination of obscenities, abusive shouts, and war whoops. Then out of nowhere Lisa and Donna appeared at Carla's side, pulling her to the very eye of the action. "Come on! Come on!" squealed Donna with obvious delight. "It's SHOWtime!"

Now as Carla observed Andy's naked cruelty at close range, she felt waves of repulsion roll over her. She knew that her alcohol induced fog was finally clearing and now without question or quibble she knew exactly whose side she was on.

Sliding an arm around her boyfriend's waist, she

gave him a gentle nudge while purposely blowing her warm moist breath into his ear. "Come on, Andy, we've got better things to do. Come on, babe, come on, let's get out of here!"

But without so much as a sideways glance, he shoved Carla away with a quick push from the palm of his hand. Then grabbing Stephan's ears, one in each of his hands, Andy began screaming into the man's face. "What's the matter with you, you fucking atheist? Don't you believe in the Bible!?"

"Yes, yes," Stephan yelled. "I *do* believe!"

Bursting with swelling masculine pride, Spider and Ironman held Stephan between them as if he were a much-prized Safari trophy.

Carla forcefully grabbed Andy's arm. "Andy, please . . . please, I have to go home now! It's getting late. We promised my mother—remember?"

If looks could kill, then the frozen stare that he now fixed on her was capable of dispensing instant death. Between clenched teeth, he warned, "Back off! Way off! Carla, get away now."

Grinning like a winning warrior, Andy barked out commands while Ironman and Spider held Stephan's arms securely behind his back.

"What are you, some kind of infidel who laughs at Jesus Christ Our Lord and Savior?" demanded an irate Andy, while twisting his captive's ears as though they were easily replaceable parts.

"No! No!" yelled Stephan, his voice splintered by a combination of fears and tears. "I'm not—not an atheist! I studied for the priesthood! Two years for the—oh, please let me go. Please! I never hurt anybody . . . I never hurt . . ." Sobs began to rack his slight body and for some moments he was unable to speak.

Andy's words came out with a surprising softness. "Hey, that's okay. You can cry if you want to, but when you're ready to talk we're here ready and able to listen. Now what could be fairer than that?"

With an effort borne of desperation, the defeated Stephan sucked back tears to start again. "I studied for the priesthood . . . Weston School of Theology. I'm a man of God . . . never in my life hurt anybody, so why are you hurting me? Why???"

"You think that surprises me?" Andy queried while returning to a strident tone. "All those priests running around wearing their long, black dresses? You think I don't know why? 'Cause they're all faggots—why else would they wear dresses? And that goes double, triple for your pope. Pope . . . pope—what's his name?"

Stephan had to stifle back sobs before he was capable of answering. "John Paul. Pope John Paul the Second."

Andy spat from the side of his mouth. "And that's what I think of your Mary-worshipping fag of a pope. You think God is just kidding around when he said: And if a man lays down with a man the same way he lays down with a woman, both have committed an A-BOM-IN-A-TION!"

"Andy could you please make him open up his eyes?" Donna politely requested. "My mother says you can always tell a fag by his eyes."

"You heard the lady!" Andy drawled, putting heavy accent on the word *lady*. "Go ahead and open your eyes, faggot!"

Obediently Stephan's eyes popped open, but there wasn't enough visibility under the existing moonlight for either Donna or Lisa to make a "fair judgment." So Stephan was half dragged, half escorted by Spider and the Ironman to the front of the Oldsmobile where the high beams still shone. Because the auto's lights were too concentrated for Stephan to keep his eyes open for more than a blink, Andy obligingly held them apart while Donna and Lisa took their time looking deep into the man's earth-brown eyes. "Well, I guess he looks enough like a guy in his eyes all right," Donna allowed after some thoughtful consideration. "But I sure do wonder . . . I wonder if he looks like a guy *everywhere*?"

"Everywhere?" Andy asked, clearly perplexed.

"Well, you know," Lisa joined in, attempting to help out. "Oh, come on, Andy, don't be *entirely* stupid—in the one and only place that guys *really* look like guys."

Andy blinked as though somebody had given him an unexpected sock on the jaw, then grinned. "Well, I guess in the name of scientific research we could find out. Okay, men, pull down the prisoner's pants!"

As both Spider and Ironman glanced at their leader's face to check if he was really serious, Andy began shrieking at them. "Do it! Do it!!!!"

At first hesitantly, Spider followed by Ironman began fumbling with their captive's silver belt buckle as a screaming and kicking Stephan begged, "No, no, please, Dei Mater! No! No! Don't let them do this to me, please, please Dei Mater!!!"

All at once, Carla lunged forward and shoved Spider and Ironman off balance and out of the way while managing to skillfully wedge herself between Andy and his prey. "All right, Andy! All right!" she spoke between zippered teeth. "If the others won't tell you, then I will! You have no right, no right at all to do this to another human being! Enough is enough! You've had your fun! Now let him go!"

"Know what's wrong with you, Carla?" Andy spoke evenly and seemingly without a trace of anger, and it was just that evenness that gave his words added authority. "You wouldn't know a real soldier for Christ if you fell over him. But hey," he exclaimed, raising his hands in a sign of surrender, "that's not your fault, and I don't blame you for it either. Considering that your own mother is the town atheist who had the gall to argue against Rachetville erecting a manger scene, well, then how could *anybody* expect you to understand the least little thing about *true* Christian ethics? You ought to get down on your knees and thank God that at least you were born pretty."

The next moment the only sound was from the rushing of clean, mountain air racing into Carla's lungs. The tension from that silence was almost unbearable until her strong index finger suddenly jutted forward. "Who the hell are you to put *my* mother down?" She poked at Andy's chest and looked at him with withering disgust. How could she have fallen for someone so cruel? "If you weren't so damn ignorant then you'd know that Plato and Aristotle were teaching ethics to the Greeks hundreds of years before the birth of Christ. As far as comparing ethics, yours to my mother's— that's a joke! She's the jolly green giant and you— you're an ethical pygmy—no, an insect. Yes, yes an insect, an ethical insect 'cause only someone that small"—she flicked the tip of a polished fingernail— "would gang up on an innocent man."

"Innocent?!!" Andy thundered. "Can't you see *any-thing*? I'm giving you a chance, Carla. I'm telling you, he's breaking God's law."

"You mean, it's God's law that he's breaking?" she asked indredulously.

"Yes!" he boomed. "God's law!"

"But, Andy, you believe—you've *told* me that you believe that God is all powerful!"

"God *is* all powerful."

Carla shook her head as though somewhere a lie was lurking. "If you really believed that then you'd allow God to punish Stephan Jones."

"Can't you get it through your thick but pretty head—he's a faggot?" Andy's outstretched hands seemed to Carla to almost be begging her for understanding at the same time he unintentionally sprayed her with fine spit. "A friggin', fucking faggot!"

"I'm pleading with you—please! Let him go, Andy. Please. Nobody elected you ruler of the world! So please, please just let him go!"

Andy released a great sigh followed by an even greater pause—he seemed to be mentally adding, subtracting, and doing a final tallying up of the scores: What would be the losses if he continued the bashing? What would be the losses if he relented, letting Stephan go? Would he lose his status with the others? It seemed to boil down to keeping the fairy and teaching him a lesson he wouldn't forget or keeping Carla, his only real girlfriend. She was the one girl he could never forget. Who would have believed that it would come down to choosing between Carla and a faggot?

"Okay, okay." His words had a weariness about them, and yet more of a softness than she had dared hope for. "Get back into the Olds, Carla. I'll be there."

Feeling a tremendous sense of relief, she knew that she must say absolutely nothing to provoke him further now he had publicly done an about-face. At least allow him a little face-saving, she told herself. "I'll wait for you in the car," she announced matter-of-factly. She then turned and without once looking behind her, walked straight to the Olds where she slid onto the passenger seat and slammed the door behind her.

Although she noticed Andy steering everybody across the bridge and farther away from the strong glare of the automobile's lights and deeper and deeper into the privacy of the darkness, Carla was not exactly worried. Knowing Andy, she figured that just once more he had to appear blazingly macho before keeping his word and finally allowing Stephan Jones to go free.

The minutes, or maybe they were merely seconds, went by. They went by so slowly Carla wished she had on a watch. How long had she been there, sitting alone in Andy's car? Once she heard Lisa's high-pitched voice taunting Stephan: "Baby! Baby! You're nothing but a baby!"

Lisa's cruelty was almost more difficult for Carla to understand than Andy's because for some reason she only dimly understood, Andy Harris was spooked senseless by Stephan Jones and Frank Montgomery. It was as though he believed that his very maleness would be increased by stripping Stephan of his. Although the logic escaped Carla, she knew that Andy's contorted beliefs convinced him that what he had been doing was justified.

But Lisa, Lisa Crowell, what could be her excuse? So did you rummage around searching for that little void within the man that could stand a bit more pain? So you did your thing and supplied it. Well, well, how very thoughtful of you, Lisa Lee Crowell!

Without a watch and *with* only an overwrought nervous system to guide her, Carla couldn't be sure how much time had passed. But even so, it felt as though it had been a long wait. After all, how long does it take for a red-blooded Rachetville boy to demonstrate how really heroic he is?

But Carla was afraid that getting out of the car

again, checking things out, wouldn't be smart, not a bit! For it could rekindle the rage that Andy had already so nicely simmered down. On the other hand, what if he didn't see her? What if she first unscrewed the bulb that automatically went on whenever the door opened? And what if she then opened the car door without bothering to slam it closed and went to check?

In the next minute, she was tiptoeing her way through the darkness toward the sounds and shapes of Andy's semicircle, and when she heard his easy flowing laughter, she felt greatly comforted. So much so that she began wondering if Stephan hadn't already been sent (shaken, but basically unharmed) on his way.

As she soundlessly stood there, considering whether or not it would be okay to rejoin the group or slip back into the car unobserved, something happened to change everything. Lisa, helpful-as-ever Lisa, pointed out an ugly rip on the jacket of Andy's rented tux.

"Look! Look what you've done!" thundered Andy as he began punching the helpless man. "My daddy will kill me for this, and it's all your fault, you son of a bitch!!!"

Carla saw that Andy was clearly out of control. Nobody could successfully interrupt his rage. Whatever she tried to do now could only make him and it worse. Seeing him battering an already physically and mentally beaten man told her that the fragile fragments of control that Andy had regained moments before had totally deserted him. Deserted him on the mere tear of a tuxedo sleeve!

She had to get help and get it fast! The keys were still in the ignition, and driving the Olds probably wouldn't be totally different from driving her mother's old stick-shift Volvo. Only now—damn—they had all moved too close to the car!

Kicking off her three-inch heels and grabbing up as much of her ankle-length skirt in her arms as possible, she began running in her stocking feet back across the bridge, back toward the closer town, back toward Parson Springs.

But before she had even reached the end of the bridge, her bare feet had already endured punishment from roadside debris, mostly small-to-medium-sized rocks. Each time an unprotected foot struck one of those painfully hard objects, her instinct was to slow down at least long enough to nurse her hurt. Momentarily hopping on one foot, she cradled the wounded limb in her hands while promising that she'd make no more concessions to pain. Had to keep moving . . . faster forward . . . faster forward. No matter what, 'cause the only thing that mattered was getting help before Stephan Jones got mutilated.

Once across the bridge, Carla began running along the narrow grassy stretch that paralleled the road, and while that was easier on her feet, she had another problem. Her breath was now coming in short jabs. And soon her body was constantly demanding that she stop and rest. *Rest, rest,* it pleaded, if only for a moment. But instead of resting, she remembered Andy's handsome face contorted into hideousness by hatred that raged beyond his ability to control.

She stumbled forward, and beads of perspiration rolled down her forehead and onto her cheeks as her eyes scanned the wooded area along the left-hand side of the highway. Somewhere on this side of the road, back there mostly hidden by the leafy summer foliage, she remembered seeing a house. Actually, she wasn't even certain she had ever seen it. But she had seen its rural mailbox a month or two or three ago. She remembered riding by that mailbox because tied to its post was a festive bouncing-in-the-afternoon-breeze bouquet of blue and silver helium balloons.

Then in the distance, but not very far in the distance, there was something on the side of the road that looked as though it could possibly—quite possibly—be a mailbox. She told herself two things: Don't despair if it isn't and, whatever it is or isn't, don't, *don't* stop running. Never, never stop running. 'Cause it has to be along here somewhere, along here. She didn't dream it, certainly not the helium balloons!

With the abundant skirt of her party dress that she held in her arms, she wiped the heavy moisture that rippled down her face. Now, as each tortured step took her closer and closer, she didn't think there was any mistake about it. Thank God! It really was what she prayed it would be: a mailbox. In a burst of speed that she did not know she was capable of, she turned at the mailbox, and with her last ounce of energy sprinted up the driveway to the quietly sleeping bungalow.

Chapter 18

On the Bridge, Spider grasped the prisoner's wrists and Ironman grasped his feet. They began swinging a totally distraught Stephan Jones back and forth, back and forth like a burlap bag of potatoes. All the while, Donna, Lisa, and Andy were laughingly revising and updating a version of one of their favorite childhood rhymes:

> Fairy, Fairy . . . quite contrary,
> How does your garden grow?
> With silver bells and cocksucking infidels
> And fucking fairies all in a row. . . ."

As the young men roughly set down their captive on the bridge's roadway, Donna whined into Andy's ear, "Did you forget all about us finding out whether or not he's a HE downstairs, where it really matters? Or are you just a little too afraid to do that?"

"Afraid?" roared Andy. "Who's afraid? You think I'm afraid of a queer!? Strip the bastard!" He screamed as though his soldiers needed hearing aids. "Strip him I say!"

This time neither Spider nor Ironman wasted a moment checking Andy's face for confirmation, for this time they knew exactly what to do. With a precision that would have done a drill team proud, they went to it, straight to it.

If Stephan had previously fought the good fight to save his modesty, then it was only a pale copy of the ferociousness of the battle he now waged. Although his hands and legs were secured by the two strong members of Andy's army, he lunged his body from side to side, snapping his teeth like a caged and crazed animal.

When Andy and the girls began to work his silver belt buckle, Stephan threw back his head and shrieked, "Dei Mater! Help me! Please! Please! Dei Mater!" In spite of his desperate wailings, it neither brought the divine intervention of the Mother of God nor did it touch the heart of any of the five elegantly attired young people.

Together, Andy and Donna pulled off Stephan's right shoe. They laughingly called out "one potato" as it went sailing high over the railing and sang out "two potato" as the left one followed.

Then, when Andy and the girls managed to grab the waist of Stephan's trousers, Andy waited until Donna unbuttoned them, with her thumb and index finger delicately bringing the zipper all the way down to its base. Not until then did their commandant commence counting: "One . . . two . . . three . . . DOWN!" With everyone pulling together, the trousers were dragged all the way down to the prisoner's ankles. "HOORAY!" In unison, the mighty cheer went up, but even so it could not entirely drown out the deeper groans of pain and humiliation.

The only thing saving Stephan Jones from total waist-down nakedness was a pair of white jockey shorts that hugged his body like a second skin.

Again Andy began the countdown as he and the girls clutched at the underwear's elastic waistband. "One . . . two . . . three . . . DOWN!!!" This time as Stephan was exposed in all his bareness, the whoops and cheers of victory were louder and more triumphant than before, but the anguished moans and groans of defeat were more terrible than before.

The curious five crowded around the prostate and quaking Stephan Jones to look down upon a long, but limp penis resting against a backdrop of pale pubic hair. Although they were mercilessly observing the most private part of his body, Stephan kept his eyes clamped closed. It was as though his last scrap of pride was tied up in his steadfast refusal to set eyes upon the faces of those who humiliated, tormented, and defiled him.

As they wordlessly observed Stephan's genitals, anger began to rise up within the boys that was both unexplained and unexpected. The problem was, although they needed to find something that marked Stephan as an inferior male, the evidence they searched for just wasn't there. Andy, like his men, believed there would, by necessity, be clean, clear lines of demarcation between splendid he-men specimens like themselves and limp-wristed fairies like Stephan Jones.

Finally it was Doug's girl, Donna, who broke the silence. "Boy, aren't they something else? Damn if those aren't the biggest dingdong-a-lings I've ever seen *and* that's a fact!"

Suddenly the Ironman, with his cheeks puffed in anger, gave Donna a watch-your-tongue pop on the arm before issuing his first-ever command: "Okay, that's enough of that! Get some clothes on that faggot before I puke!"

"Wait a fucking minute! Not so fast!" countermanded the *real* leader. "Seeing as how Stephan here is almost ready for a little skinny-dipping, maybe that's what he'd enjoy doing." Andy's voice then dropped to a lower, more intimate register. "That right, Stephanie? You want to go for a refreshing little swim?"

Stephan's eyes popped wide open. *"What?!"*

"Oh, I just thought you'd enjoy a swim."

"No! No! Please! PLEASE! Listen to me. I'm begging you—I don't know how to swim! I can't swim! I *never* learned to swim!"

Andy shook his head slowly, but firmly, a little reminiscent of a kindly old family doctor who's about to insist that, for the patient's own good, the nasty-tasting medicine must be swallowed. "Oh, you shouldn't ever say *can't* 'cause I believe you can swim. Everybody can swim. At least every *real* man can swim."

All five snickered knowingly as Andy barked out the orders for Spider and Ironman to "take up your positions at the north and south of the prisoner."

"No! No! Honest, you've got to believe me! No! Don't do this! DON'T!!!" Spider and the Ironman again began to slowly swing the frantic man. "I'm aquaphobic!"

"Oh, bless your precious little heart," Donna cooed, attempting to imitate the sounds of sympathy.

The five's robust laughter was an eerie counterpoint to Stephan's screams for mercy.

"I'm terrified of water! Please, please, oh, please, I'm begging you, don't do this!!!"

But the closest thing to an answer they gave him was their mocking laughter. That and the swings—the ever-higher swinging back and forth. With tears running down his cheeks Stephan cried out, "Oh, Dei Mater! Mother of God. Blessed Mary Mother of God, help me, HELP ME!!!"

For a moment Ironman's broad features registered indecision and discomfort. "Andy, hey, like what if the guy's telling the truth? What if he really *can't* swim?"

Andy scoffed. "That's a bold-faced lie." He turned to throw him a look of disgust, reminding Doug that he himself had been swimming ever since his old man threw him into Baxter Pond when he was five.

The Ironman's well-developed arms began to lose the momentum of their swing as he asked Andy again, "Yeah, but what if this one *really* can't swim?"

"What if! What if!" lambasted Andy. "What if you're not one of *us,* but one of *them*? What if you're not an Ironman but only a half man? What about that, eh?!"

Andy and the Ironman's eyes connected, and then Doug looked away as he once again began to fall into the rhythm of the swing.

Like a sheet caught hanging on a clothesline during an unexpected storm, Stephan was now whipped back and forth, back and forth, and with each swing his half-naked body was falling and rising. Faster and faster, higher and higher. "Oh, help me! Help me! Blessed Mary Mother of God! Help me! Help me! Blessed Mary Mother of God! I CAN'T SWIM!!!"

With Stephan's body approaching the height of the guardrail, Lisa, remembering a now obscenely appropriate nursery rhyme, began singing with a honey-sweet soprano voice. Immediately the others joined in, and with surprisingly good harmony the handsome party-goers swung and sang into the night:

Rock-a-bye baby,
In the treetops
When the wind blows,
The cradle will rock,
When the bough breaks,
The cradle will fall,
And down will come baby
Cradle and all.

As they sang out the words, Stephan Jones was sent sailing up and over the bridge's iron railing, up, up into the moonlit sky, crying and calling, calling and crying, "BLESSEDMARYMOTHEROFGODPRAYFOR USNOWANDATTHETIMEOFOURDEATH." His anguished cries pierced the otherwise silent night.

As Stephan screamed his tortured cries heavenward, "BLESSEDMAR—" there was a splash, and he slipped soundlessly beneath the moving waters.

With their heads bowed over the railings, the five formally attired promgoers stared almost transfixed at the dark and brooding water of the Pascaloosa below. Wordlessly five sets of eyes scanned the river for a sign of life. They watched as the moments became minutes and the minutes ticked by.

Suddenly Donna broke the collective trance by asking, "Hey, isn't it about time for him to come up for air?"

Nobody answered, they merely continued to gaze at the river and feel the passage of time. The passage of more and more time.

"Maybe . . ." Doug sputtered, "maybe he was telling

the truth. Why wouldn't you believe him, Andy! He told you he couldn't swim!"

Andy Harris's voice spewed venom. "Oh, come on, you mean to tell me that he's got you believing that a grown man could actually drown in that *little* river? Why, he's down there laughing at you, hiding from you! Man, don't you know *anything*?"

In the distance the not-quite-of-this-earth wail of a siren startled the five so severely that they dumbly sought each other's reassurance, hoping that someone would explain that what they were hearing was just some strange group hallucination. But instead of the siren going away, it grew louder and more insistent. One of them yelled, "Let's get out of here!"

They were all running, running like a flock of frightened chickens back to the Olds, and even as the ignition was turned on and the car was lurching forward, the back doors were being slammed closed. Jerking the Olds into drive, Andy glanced to his right and then to the rear seat before calling, "Carla! Hey, where is she?"

"Drive!" Spider demanded. "Just DRIVE!"

Andy's right foot pushed hard against the accelerator and the big car roared across the Pascaloosa, but just as they reached the opposite side, he stomped hard against the brake. Coming up on them were lights, flashing emergency lights.

Then, like an ace fighter pilot who knows precisely when it's time to turn tail and run, Andy spun the automobile around and once again struck out across the bridge. No sooner were they gunning for the opposite bank did the terrible truth begin to crash down upon them. Not only were they being hotly pursued from behind, but there were also sirens and flashing lights coming toward them. "Oh-h-h, no-o-o," Andy moaned, bringing the sedan to an abrupt stop. "That other one! That other son of a bitch, son of a whore faggot! He did it! He brought the cops!"

With his fist, Ironman struck his own forehead as though he were finally trying to knock some life into brain cells that had long since died. "Why did I listen to you? I should have fucking known better than to listen to you, Andy! My folks are going to kill me! *Kill* me!"

"Well, I *sure* didn't have anything to do with it," interjected his pretty prom date, looking horrified that anyone could, even for a moment, consider pointing an accusatory finger at her. "Now you all know that's so!"

"And neither did I!" sweetly sang out Lisa as though she were the lead singer in a celestial choir.

With his bare fists, Andy violently banged the steering wheel. "Shut up! Can't you see we're all in this thing together? Don't you stupid asses understand anything at *all*?" The ever-louder and more piercing wail of the sirens, both behind and in front of them, made the five feel as though they had been helplessly snared into a trap that was not of their making.

The double wailing sirens made it necessary for Andy to raise his voice and shout, "Listen to me! We—none of us—had anything to do with that faggot jumping off the bridge, understand that? Remember the *only* reason we're here at all was to ask those queers to quit the lewd screwing they were doing out on the bridge, where anybody—even young kids and all—could see them. So that's the only reason we stopped—got that? Get it!"

Then amid flashing lights, screeching brakes, and the migraine-producing whine of its unrelenting siren, a police cruiser with the ironic lily of the valley crest of Parson Springs, Arkansas, came to an attention-getting stop directly behind the Olds.

"This is Chief Marino," called out an electrically amplified voice from inside the cruiser. "Everybody out of the car, keep your hands up, nice and easy now. Nobody's going to get hurt."

But even as the young people reluctantly piled out of the luxurious automobile, Chief Marino, with his uniformed deputy at his side, was already out of the cruiser, throwing questions at them. "Hear you all have been beating up on a man tonight. Where is he?"

"Beating up on who?" Andy replied, answering the question with a question of his own while smiling his most winning smile.

"Son, don't go getting me in a bad mood," cautioned the chief, his voice almost a full octave lower than Andy's. "The game is simple enough. It's played this way: I ask a question; you answer that question, now you got that?"

But in the next moments, the second cruiser, this one bearing the name as well as the insignia of the town of Rachetville, Arkansas, roared to the scene of the crime.

Throwing open the door and leaping from the back-seat, a frantic Frank Montgomery charged through the sparse scattering of people. It was hard to believe that he was wearing the same clothes that looked so crisp on him at the beginning of the evening. Now his suit coat was wet with perspiration, and the neck of his shirt looked ripped open. His linen trousers, with their combination of caked mud and dried blood, hinted most vividly at the nightmare that he was living.

Grabbing Andy by the elegant lapels of his rented

dinner jacket, he jerked him forward, screaming, "Where is he?! What have you done with Stephan?"

Andy squeaked something unintelligible while looking pleadingly over at Chief Marino for help, but the only response was an agonizingly slow but expressive shrug of the chief's broad shoulders, which nobody present had the slightest difficulty interpreting.

As soon as Andy realized that there was no help forthcoming, he began to quickly and loudly squawk. "Nothing! We did nothing to him! Hey, we were just horsing around, having a little fun. Look, it's my graduation prom night! Don't you think we deserve a little fun?"

"Where is he?" Frank exploded, his hands moving up from Andy's jacket to his throat. "Answer or, so help me, I'll wring your neck!"

Andy's Adam's apple bobbed up and down before his head gestured toward the river. "We were just having fun—nobody asked him to dive in, as Jesus Christ is my witness! Nobody! Honest!"

"Oh-h-h, my God! My God!" Frank's voice cracked with heartfelt anguish. "Where did he go over? *When?*"

Helpfully Andy pointed a trembling finger toward the center of the river. "Not long, only a few minutes. He surprised us all by diving in over there, about midstream."

Kicking off his shoes, Frank hand-vaulted over the rusted iron railing, but it was Andy's voice that accompanied him on his leap into the waters below. "Hey, I don't know why he jumped! Nobody asked him to—as Jesus is my witness!"

As soon as Frank's head emerged, he treaded water as he furiously turned his body around and around in a circle, calling out, "Stevie! STEVIE! STEVIE!" But he heard no response, no human voice at all except the sharply staccato shrieks of denial from Andy that kept echoing down to him from the bridge. "Nobody asked him to go swimming! Nobody!

Ducking again and again and still again below the black-brown waters, Frank attempted through the sheer force of his will *and* his need to command his eyes to see what they could not possibly see. No matter how desperately he tried, his eyes could not penetrate the cold and murky waters.

Stretching out his hands and legs, Frank kept praying, praying, always praying that the next reaching out and grabbing would be the one that reached out and grabbed Stevie, grabbed Stevie alive, grabbed Stevie alive and well.

Skipping and shimmering across the river's dimpled surface were dollops of lights from two or three hand-held spotlights. Also from topside came the radio-transmitted voices that, between bursts of static, could be heard calling for emergency personnel and equipment.

Emerging from a radio-dispatched ambulance, two uniformed attendants raced down the embankment pushing a stretcher. The next person to arrive wasn't one of the emergency personnel at all, but Eddie Jameson, the editor of the weekly *Rachetville Banner,* wearing his red-and-white candy-striped pajama top under his buff-colored windbreaker.

Back on the bridge, a great white van with the call letters WABT-TV EYEWITNESS NEWS was attempting to park on the bridge in spite of a sheriff's deputy who angrily waved it on.

A few hundred yards below on the east bank of the river, Chief Marino with spotlight in hand paced nervously back and forth while barking out orders to Pete, his slender, eager young officer, who was working the radio transmitter. With his bullhorn, he spoke to the lone man in the water. "Frank Montgomery, I want you out of the water! You've already been in there too long. Divers are on their way from Fayetteville, Harrison, and Fort Smith, and a police helicopter should be here momentarily. Come on out now, you hear?"

To the lawman's surprise, he saw Frank Montgomery turn his pain-wracked body around in the water and stop. No more dunking under, coming up, and dunking under again. He stopped, and finally, with dead-dog weariness, began his labored swim back toward the riverbank.

Chapter 19

BY THE TIME the cool, coral dawn burst brilliantly over Crowley's Ridge, Frank Montgomery, with a Red Cross blanket draped haphazardly across his shoulders, was sitting alone on the dried-mud bank of the Pascaloosa. With unblinking eyes, he stared transfixed at the river. But however hard he stared, it was uncertain if he was actually seeing or merely seeing through what was happening: the team of divers in wet suits going in and out of the water; the Parson Springs police chief mapping out likely places in the river to continue the search. The Red Cross volunteers were handing out hot coffee and warm blankets to all of the emergency personnel. It was amid this nuts-and-bolts rescue mission that Frank's anguish stood out in startlingly high relief.

The continuous picture show of his mind was playing and replaying, not what was happening around him, but what had happened at the precise moment, at that never-to-be-forgotten or forgiven moment, five hours before. If only he could, he would have happily given everything he was, everything he would be, everything he owned or would ever have—if only he could change, change what he did for what he should have done. Sick with grief as well as thick with shame, he couldn't help wondering why he'd split and gone racing off in the opposite direction from Stevie.

Why did he have to recall his ROTC training commands for defense? If only . . . if only they had stayed together, standing together and fighting together, fighting like hell!

By seven A.M. there was no need to question the power of the electronic media, for the bridge had taken on a Sunday parade atmosphere. Lines of honking cars and mud-splashed pickup trucks clogged the lanes and within each vehicle were stretched-neck curiosity seekers who'd heard the news.

As the angry chief observed the spectacle on the bridge, he despaired that his deputies could never keep the home traffic flowing freely. Stalking up the embankment, he positioned the electric bullhorn in front of his lips: "This is Chief Marino warning you all! It is necessary that we keep this traffic moving. This bridge must be kept open for emergency vehicles! This is a warning! All traffic *must* be kept moving!"

Len Bassett adjusted his red GMC baseball-style cap before shouting out, "Chet—hey! Did you all find that queer's body yet?"

Chet Marino placed a hand on his hip as he brought the bullhorn back to his lips so that not just Len, but everybody on the bridge could hear. "This is not a sideshow, Bassett! A man is missing and feared drowned.

If you can't show a little respect then I pity you. Get the hell out of here, all of you!"

Up and down the elevated roadway, people returned to their cars like scared turtles retreating to the safety of their shells. The chief's brass buttons glinted in the midmorning sun as he threw brisk and authoritative hand signals to move on.

From his vantage point on the river's bank, Frank Montgomery observed another pair of obviously disappointed divers being pulled back onto a flat-bottom boat. And as he watched still more divers come up without having found Stephan's body, an idea began nipping at him. At first, it was merely that, a small nibble, but gradually it began taking larger and larger bites of his thoughts: the idea that maybe, just maybe, Stephan hadn't drowned at all.

The water was only six or seven feet, and that was at its deepest. If Stephan had actually drowned, wouldn't they have located his body by now?

Frank began to speculate with gathering conviction that a totally traumatized Stephan was still out there hiding in the woods. Stevie was only waiting until the morning, until the full light of morning seeped through the leafy forest ceiling and then, only then, he'd feel safe enough to find his way home.

A middle-aged woman wearing the familiar and reassuring shoulder patch of the American Red Cross brought Frank a Styrofoam cup filled with steaming black coffee. As he accepted the cup, she dropped an arm around his shoulder. "Up near our van, we've set up some cots, Frank. Why don't you lie down, rest for a while?"

"Rest?" repeated Frank while looking up at her with eyes that were rimmed with red. "No thank you . . .

not now," he exclaimed while suddenly throwing off his blanket and rising quickly to his feet. With long strides, he headed for the line of trees, broke into a jog, and finally began to sprint.

Once inside the shadowy domain of trees and under-brush, Frank cupped his hands around his mouth. "Stevie! Stevie! Hey, Stevie, where are you?" Training his ears to hear more keenly than they had ever been asked to hear before, he listened intently for sounds. For his effort he could only catch the squawking of a couple of discontented crows.

Making his way deeper and deeper into the forest's interior, he listened for sounds that were altogether familiar and altogether human. "Ste-vie! Ste-vie! Ste-vie, you don't have to be afraid anymore," he called encouragingly. "Come on! Out of your hiding, Stevie! It's only me! Only Frank. All your enemies have been taken away. You're safe, Stevie! Nobody will ever hurt you again. I promise I'll never let anyone hurt you again."

He came upon a spot where a Plymouth Rock–sized stone protruded from the earth. A person could wedge himself up under that slightly uplifted boulder and beneath that impenetrable rock and feel hidden, secure, and safe from all danger.

As his eyes searched the damp, smoke-colored inte-rior for signs of life, Frank could see little—but his heart beat faster as he heard breathing. The steady inhaling . . . exhaling . . . inhaling . . . exhaling coming from the hiding place. Sticking his head still deeper into the shadowy interior, he softly called, "Stevie? Hey, Stevie, it's me—it's Frankie!"

"Ook-suwee-ook-suey-suey!" It sounded like someone in the middle of an asthma attack. There was a rush

and a blur of pink and gray, and a wild pig—a mad-as-hell razorback—was flushed from his home! Watching the critter race off into the woods filled Frank with despair. So much despair that it took all of his persuasive powers to keep from sliding into his pit of irreversible grief. He tried to encourage himself by thinking that because that particular breathing didn't turn out to be Stephan's, it didn't prove a thing!

Frank walked on spongy bog grasses past clinging vines of honeysuckle that filled the morning air with a pungent sweetness impossibly at odds with his own sadness and racking fears. Thinking negatively meant giving in to grief, to believing that Stephan had drowned. Frank knew—he just knew that he hadn't, because any fool could tell that Stephan was only . . . only hiding.

Frank followed a path dictated by his will-o'-the-wisp intuition. Tramping past pine, elm, and birches, he followed the river on his hard-to-figure, helter-skelter route. From time to time, he'd come to a dead stop to halt the noisy snapping of dried branches and the rustling of dried leaves underfoot. Then he'd just stand quiet to listen for any sounds that might turn out to be human sounds. Stevie's sound!

When Frank was satisfied that there were no noises worth investigating, he'd call out so Stephan would know that there was nobody there but him. "Hey, fella, it's just me. Everything's okay now. You don't have to be afraid—I won't let anybody hurt you, not ever again! If you're afraid, you don't have to come out of hiding, Stevie. Just call my name—call out my name and I'll come to you. I promise I'll come to you!"

Every time Frank called out to Stephan and waited for an answer—for an answer that never came—he felt as though that spiteful silence had plunged a spike directly through his aorta. Frank began to talk to himself. "Hey, just because Stevie hasn't heard me up to now doesn't mean he won't hear. No answer doesn't mean that at the next bend of the river, or maybe the next bend after that, I won't get my answer.

"Sometimes, and I know this to be true, things turn out better than anyone would have believed. What about that time I had forgotten my cherished outfielder's mitt—the one autographed by the great Yastrzemski himself—on the park bench at Dean Park. I begged Dad to drive me back to the park and he said he would, but he made me promise not to get my hopes up because that mitt had as much chance of still being there as 'a snowball in hell.' Well, chalk one up for snowballs because it was there, there exactly where I had left it. Certainly Stephan could have walked out of a shallow river and hidden in the forest. No, no miracle in that because it is the most logical explanation possible."

But how real, he asked himself, is an act of faith unless you keep right on demonstrating that faith. So, filling his lungs with air, he cupped his hands around his mouth and called in the direction of the river. "Stevie! Stevie! Come on now . . . there's nobody here to hurt you. It's only me . . . ON-LY ME! Please, Stevie, please just let me know you're here. Please call my name . . . oh . . . please, all you have to do is call my name."

Then suddenly, totally unexpectedly, against the floor of the forest, there was a breaking and cracking of branches. At first Frank was terrified that his senses were playing dirty tricks on him and that he was "hearing" only what he so desperately needed to hear. But no—no, there it was again, brittle limbs and twigs cleanly snapping under the feet of a large something or someone running this way. In the direction of the commotion, he cried out joyously, "Here, Stevie! Here! I'm here!!!"

Then every bit as miraculously as some of those Bible miracles of old, he heard a young man's voice clearly echoing through the otherwise still woods: "Frank! Hey, Frank!" When he heard his name being called, Frank's hand rushed to his heart. It was as though he were frightened that his heart would literally splinter apart with happiness. Then raising his arms heavenward, Frank raced frantically toward the voice while crying loudly enough to terrorize all the creatures of the forest, "Here! Here! Stevie! Stevie! I'm here!!!"

But the person who stepped through the partial clearing to face Frank Montgomery was not Stephan Jones! It was the officer in the smart blue uniform from the Parson Springs Police Department. "Uh, Frank, uh, Chief Marino sent me to bring you back."

Frank stared at the officer as though he had never before actually seen a man wearing a uniform. "I can't go back, not yet," he finally explained. "Not until I find Stevie."

"The chief wants you, Frank. You must come. Please, it's best."

"I *already* told you that I can't! Not until I find Stevie!"

"I'm really sorry to tell you this, Frank, but Stephan Jones has already been found. The chief wants you to come identify the body."

Frank listened without really hearing, or at least without giving even the slightest indication he had understood what he had heard. Then, his face took on a puzzled look. Finally he smiled and began shaking his head no. "Whoever it is you've found, it's certainly not Stevie!" he stated emphatically. Then Frank affected a lifeless laugh, as if he were trying desperately to convince himself even more than the officer. "Definitely not Stevie! Hey, no way!"

"Well come on with me, anyway, okay, Frank?"

"I *can't*—don't you understand!? I've got to stay here, search for Stevie!"

"Frank, listen to me, please. Come back to the command post with me and if the man the divers found isn't Stevie then I'll come back here to the woods with you and help you search—we all will!"

The dazed man slowly nodded his agreement before following. At first Frank's trek back seemed mechanical, almost robotic, but as his fear began to expand, his pace, too, began to quicken, until in the final stretch he was running. By the time they reached sight of the base, the perspiration was rolling in rivulets down Frank's body.

At the disaster scene, people with badges on their chests and official-looking patches on their sleeves stood around. Divers were being helped out of their rubber suits. With a sense of hopeless finality, a seasoned emergency medical technician slammed down the plastic lid on his fibrillator. A few feet away, Chief Marino was giving an impromptu press conference for reporters. But by far the largest hub of humanity was clustered around a stretcher, its shiny chrome wheels reflecting the rays of the newly risen sun.

As Frank raced forward, most people seemed to respectfully back away from him. The group stepped back from the stretcher, revealing a blue-gray blanket that covered a decidedly human shape. Frank stood staring at the blanketed form as though he were the master of all time, all the time in the world. Then, with a trembling hand, he finally reached out to turn back the cover.

The face beneath the blanket appeared to be the cruel prank of a particularly sadistic cartoonist, for it didn't look nearly as much like Stephan Jones as like a hideously grotesque version of Stephan Jones. His pale porcelain skin had taken on a bluish cast and the once well-defined planes and valleys of his sculptured face were hideously swollen. And those hazel eyes, which only yesterday were alive with life, were closed, closed now and closed for all eternity.

Frank gasped like a stabbed animal, and it was a gasp that carried unspeakable agony! Frank dropped to Stephan's side, crying out, "Oh, my God! My God! My God!" then abandoned himself to uncontrollable sobs.

Chapter 20

ALTHOUGH THE TRIAL that nationally came to be known as the "Trial of the Rachetville Five" did not actually commence until the second week in September, the summer air hung thickly with a blanket of oppressive heat. Inside the turn-of-the-century courtroom, overhead fans lazily stirred the steamy air, sluggishly moving it from one hot place to still another.

As Carla leaned forward to better hear Andy smoothly reciting his answers from the witness stand, Judith gave her daughter a couple of rapid, reassuring pats to the forearm. It was her way of letting someone she loved know and understand that whatever happened, she would always be there.

During the course of the trial, whenever Spider, Ironman, Lisa, Donna, and especially Andy could capture Carla's eye, they would throw poison arrow looks from their seats at the witness stand or their chairs at the defendants' table. Carla absorbed their disdain with barely any visible response. How many months, weeks, days ago had it been since she had craved their approval?

She speculated that Donna and Lisa must have agreed upon not only the clothes they would wear for today's session, but also exactly what expressions they'd exhibit. Their almost identical twin pouts as much as their pastel-colored suits made them look as though they had both emerged from the same birth canal.

Privately all five of the defendants blamed Carla for all their troubles with money, the law, and their families. Carla Wayland, they complained, was the fink who went and ratted on them; supposedly she was a friend. "We'll get you for it, too!" they had threatened. "We'll get you good!"

The fierce and mean-spirited glances were messages that silently cried out, "We are together. We are the still proud members of the now and forever famous Rachetville Five. Churches take up collections for us; lawyers defend us; newspapers quote us; photographers snap us; our relatives pray for us; friends embrace us; and our whole town—and yes, even far, far beyond this town—celebrate us! But you, Carla Wayland, you are an outcast.

"You, Carla, are different. You act different than folks in Rachetville. If our most deeply held beliefs aren't good enough for you to believe, then go someplace else. Why don't you find some hole under some rock where you can hide? Some place where they can stomach your liberal stuff.

"You're alone, Carla Wayland. Until our dying days, we've made each other a solemn, unbreakable promise: We're all going to stick together faster than Scotch tape while making certain that you always are all alone."

Andy's lawyer, Chip Burwick, sported slightly shaded prescription aviator glasses. His square jaw was set as he drawled, "Now, Andy, in the first place, some of us still have a little trouble understanding why you—a young man who took his obligations to his studies so seriously as well as his obligations to his family's business so seriously—would find the time or the interest to mess around with the likes of Stephan Jones."

"Well, sir, looking back now . . . it's like real hard for me to understand, too." Andy Harris was seriously suited in well-tailored navy-blue with a pale blue oxford cloth shirt and a silk tie with enough regent stripes to be cherished by an army of preppies. "I mean, one thing's for sure, we—none of us—ever *meant* to hurt him!"

Chip rapid-fired a question: "And how *do* you feel now about what actually did happen?"

"Oh, I feel very, very bad about that accident. Yes sir, I sure do. I mean there's not a day that passes that I don't feel bad about what happened, as Jesus is my witness. Know something? I'd give my own life gladly—and you can ask my dad, he'll tell you that I'd give my own life gladly if that would help bring that guy back to life."

"Well, since you obviously didn't want him to drown, what was it that you really did *mean* to do?" Chip's manner and voice was calm, reassuring, and strongly reminiscent of an older, more responsible brother lovingly helping his foolhardy sibling.

Without needing even a moment's worth of contemplation, Andy spewed forth his reply just as though the teacher were giving a pop quiz for which he had already been supplied the answers. "The only thing I wanted to do, sir, was to rough him up a little—just enough of a roughing to teach him a lesson, if you know what I mean."

"When you say you wanted to teach Stephan Jones a lesson, *exactly* what kind of a lesson did you have in mind?"

"Trying to teach him that he ought not go around flaunting his evil ways."

"Objection!" called out the chief prosecutor, Wayne Dillman. "It is not Mr. Jones who is on trial here!"

"Sustained," echoed Judge Morris Bernhardt. "Mr. Burwick, I have reminded you repeatedly, and I do not expect to remind you or your client again that this jury has not been convened to sit in judgment on the deceased Mr. Jones, now is that clear? Perfectly clear?"

"Perfectly," Chip Burwick responded, snapping to attention. "Sorry, Your Honor. Now, Andy, without characterizing Mr. Jones in any way, would you please give us the facts, the complete and unvarnished facts on how you came to be so upset by Mr. Jones."

"Well, sir, personally—even though I am a born-again Christian—I have what you might call a live-and-let-live philosophy with respect to the way other folks might want to live their lives. So I want to explain that I've never hated the sinner—never in my life, 'cause the only thing I ever hate is the sin.

"Now if a man goes in for that perverted stuff, then I think that's his business as long as he behaves himself, especially when it comes to little children. I don't think it's ever right to flaunt your homosexuality in front of little children. And that's something that I feel very strongly about . . . and that's for sure!"

Carla glanced over at Mr. Dillman, expecting to witness another one of his outbursts over Andy's suggestion of what nobody had ever suggested before: that Stephan somehow and in some way bothered small children. But if the learned prosecutor was busy doing anything at all then, it was playing with the metal clip on his A. T. Cross ballpoint pen.

Chip Burwick lifted his wire-rimmed glasses up to mid-forehead and slowly massaged the inner corners of his eyes before gazing at Andy Harris with what could pass for a heavy dose of sensitive concern. "Andy, I know what I'm going to ask you to relate next is going to be both very hard and very difficult for a red-blooded, American boy like yourself to answer, but it's important for you to show your usual spunk and explain to this court exactly what you had previously told me. How and why, precisely why, you developed this uncontrollable anger toward Stephan Jones."

Nodding his head in slow, short bobs of agreement, he replied thoughtfully, "Well, yes, sir, you sure are right about that 'cause it *is* real hard for me to talk about it."

Leaning even closer toward his client, Chip spoke in a low and intimate voice as though nobody would ever hear his words, nobody but the two of them. "I can appreciate, and it does you credit, this natural reluctance of yours to say anything bad about the deceased, but all the same, Andy, it would help immeasurably. Sort of help this court, if you will, understand how a peaceful and otherwise nonviolent, churchgoing young man like yourself was provoked into behaving in such an uncharacteristic way."

"I have done a lot of praying over it, sir, and I've asked for deliverance from my sins, and just last night

Jesus did come to me in the spirit and he told me that I have been forgiven and from that moment on, I will have complete dominion over the devil."

"Andy, please try to tell us what happened—help us understand what was the event that pushed you over the brink?"

The quiet of the courtroom seemed to grow quieter still as the judge, the jurors, and the standing-room-only spectators strained to catch the young man's words.

Andrew Anthony Harris, dampening his perfectly formed lips with his tongue, replied, "Well, what he did was . . ."

"Yes?"

"What he did was what I hated!"

"And what exactly was it that you hated?" soothed Chip.

"Well, sir, what he did was . . ."

"What, Andy, what?"

"Stephan Jones wouldn't take no for an answer! He kept on pestering me and pestering me for sex!"

There was a sudden and communal sucking in of breath before a great gasp echoed throughout the chamber. At first, even a stunned Carla wondered why she had never heard anything before about this startling piece of information. But on second thought, it began to dawn on her why, and the reason was oh-so-very simple. It had simply never happened. Never ever happened!

IT WASN'T UNTIL the fifth day of the trial, on a Thursday morning, that Carla Wayland was called to take the stand by the chief lawyer for the prosecution. This came as as much of a surprise to Carla as a karate chop across the throat. She knew, of course, that she was scheduled to be the state's star witness against her former friends, but she was also promised plenty of advance notice.

Right from the beginning, Mr. Dillman had made it a point to advise her not to go "fretting your pretty head" about testifying. Long before that happened, he had pledged, "I'm going to have you so well prepared that you're going to be like a racehorse chomping at the bit, all ready and raring to go!"

Carla hadn't felt compelled to correct the district attorney's assumption, but she knew instinctively that she'd never feel "raring to go." In spite of her officially being on the side of the prosecution, she was not so much resolved that the Rachetville Five got punished; rather, she fervently hoped that they would develop understanding about the tragedy they had committed. Without understanding, she had come to believe, nothing would change. Without understanding, the Rachetville Five, the citizens of Rachetville, as well as much of the world beyond would continue to be convinced that because Stephan Jones was a homosexual, his murder was somehow something less than murder.

Right from the opening day, the drowning of Stephan Jones was talked about by the local people in unfair terms. These "friendly, God-fearing young folks" were treated as if they'd engaged in nothing more than a foolish prank that somehow got out of hand rather than anything resembling murder. The district attorney's office received more than sixty letters' worth of pressure demanding that the state drop its case. Some of the letters were from people who identified themselves as religious, and several were from clergy who stated that these defendants were "good kids" and even went on to quote the Bible "proving" that homosexuality was sinful.

It sometimes seemed as though the local sentiments were entirely on the side of the five young people, but several letters received by the DA's office begged him not to be "either too timid or embarrassed to pursue justice just because the victim was gay." In the last paragraph of one of these letters, the Bible was also quoted. The writer made note of the sixth commandment, which states: Thou shalt not kill.

Carla was in a state of the highest possible anxiety as she wound her way across the pews of the glaring spectators toward the witness stand. Once she seated herself on that chair and swore to "tell the truth, the whole truth, and nothing but the truth," the rapid-as-a-machine-gun interrogation did nothing to help cool her down.

The man the great state of Arkansas paid to prosecute this crime shot out questions sounding as though they had been manufactured by a munitions factory. The DA's abrasive manner made Carla want to cry out to him: Hey! I'm not just a necessary evil! For God sakes, I'm *your* witness, your only eyewitness!

As she sat there high in the witness chair above everybody besides the judge, she was bound and determined to keep her eyes focused as far away as possible from Andy and the other defendants. She also needed to shield herself from looking into her mother's eyes as well, lest she see reflected there some of the selfsame terror that even now was already gnawing at huge chunks of her own heart.

Suddenly the chief prosecutor's voice shook the courtroom. "Did you not *hear* the last question put to you, Miss Wayland?"

"Hear your question?" repeated Carla, playing for a moment of time. Maybe a moment is all she needed to forge a measure of control out of the mindless confusion charging through her brain. The question, now what was it about? About Andy . . . something about Andy and Stephan . . .

"The question you were asked, Miss Wayland, was really a very simple one, so please try to concentrate. To the best of your knowledge, did Stephan Jones ever do anything to Andy or the others to account for the violence perpetrated on him?"

"I'm sorry . . . I guess I was trying to remember what it was about Stephan that made him so hated. The big thing, of course, was that Stephan Jones— was—gay. There was nothing about him that Andy didn't hate. His breathing in and his breathing out— his thinness, his paleness, everything bothered Andy. All those things at one time or another Andy mocked."

"Listen to my question," the district attorney replied. "What, if anything, did Stephan Jones do—*do*—to cause such a reaction from Andrew Harris?"

A quizzical look floated across her face. "Do?" But then, rolling in behind that uncertainty, was a kind of hard-won decisiveness. "What I have been trying to explain is that this doesn't have anything to do with anything that Stephan Jones did, but this has everything to do with what Stephan *was*!"

For three quarters of an hour, Carla answered questions as best she could. Questions regarding actions as well as the motives of the Rachetville Five. Increasingly, she felt fatigue seeping down deep into the very marrow of her bones. Three quarters of an hour wasn't such a terribly long period of time unless it is spent on a tightrope a hundred feet above the circus specta-tors. Or answering the questions of a skilled and angry prosecutor!

Although Carla thought that she and the prosecutor were supposed to be on "the same side," it was becom-ing clear to her that something between them wasn't right. The prosecutor acted the opposite of Andy's defense lawyer, who treated his client with all the respect due a Rhodes scholar. Was she doing something wrong? Wasn't she answering quickly enough? If only he'd stop cutting off her answers every time she paused, she was certain she could give him answers all right, answers that could reach beyond and beneath the superficial, way down to the very soul of the case. Why, oh why, the girl asked herself, would he go clip-ping off my answers, as though clipping off so many dirty fingernails?

The lawyers and journalists who wrote about the trial insisted that it would be the DA's devastatingly difficult job to make a homosexual neither cartoon character nor devil, but *real*. Carla had heard all about that, but frankly, she thought that nothing should be easier.

After all, Stephan was *real*! Cried *real* tears! Upon his birth wasn't he given a *real* name and upon his death wasn't that *real* earth thrown over his mahogany casket? Even now, isn't he being grieved for by real people? Family? Friends? Frank Montgomery? Why should it be so hard for anyone—even jurors—to feel that a crime, a terrible crime, had been committed?

Eddie Jameson, her mother's friend who wrote many articles about the drowning of Stephan Jones for the local newspaper, said something that she couldn't help remembering: "It's more embarrassing for a lawyer to defend a gay man's right to life than it is to defend a murderer's right to take that life."

Carla's mother had expressed worry about how her daughter would be treated on the stand, but she knew there was absolutely nothing she could do. Mr. Dillman jutted out his face within a handsbreadth of Carla's. Then, for a second that seemed endless, neither Carla nor anyone else in the entire courtroom had any idea what to expect. Except, perhaps, to expect the unexpected. Finally Mr. Dillman thrust his freshly shaven chin skyward before spitting out his final words. "I have absolutely no further questions of this witness."

Chapter 21

IF CARLA WAYLAND felt rudely and roughly treated by the top law enforcement officer of the state, then that was merely a tiny, but terrible sample of the cross-examination leveled against her by the one-hundred-fifty-dollar-an-hour legal mind hired to defend Andy Harris. To everyone who'd listen, Larry Harris bragged, "When it comes to my son, only the best legal mind in Little Rock would do."

"Miss Wayland," barked Chip Burwick. "We have all listened most attentively as you testified at considerable length how on prom night, you witnessed your five friends beating up on the victim. Frankly, it doesn't make a lot of sense."

"Yes, sir."

"Could you *please* speak up?"

With a conspicuously conscious effort, Carla this time threw her voice nearly the entire length of the room. "YES, SIR."

He exhibited a let's-be-friends smile that she immediately rejected. "It's been my experience that sometimes even people of goodwill give testimony that, on later reflection, they may come to believe is a mistake." Chip Burwick enunciated each word carefully so that there would be no mistaking precisely what it was he was saying. "And so, if you feel that your previous testimony was in any way in error, then now is the right time to correct that error by speaking up. Would you now like to make any changes in that testimony?"

"No sir, what I said before is the whole truth and nothing but the truth."

The attorney for the defense smiled as though he and he alone were privy to an especially deep and dark and delicious secret. "Very well, Miss Wayland, we'll do it your way. Do you still maintain that you could see, actually *see*, a beating taking place when you admitted that the event happened beyond the reach of the car's headlights?"

"Well, yes sir, I . . ."

Chip Burwick shook his head as though somebody was in the process of telling him a tall tale. "Mr. Cecil Sawtelle of the National Weather Service testified in that very chair—and under oath, mind you—that there was considerable cloud cover on the night in question. Couldn't you have been mistaken about what you thought you saw?"

Carla nodded as she began to wonder if that was what was wrong with her own worn and weary brain cells. Kind of foggy with cloud cover, making it difficult to think. Making it particularly difficult to think cleanly and clearly. "No, sir, I didn't make a mistake. I left the car and walked across the bridge, so I know what I saw!"

Suddenly a great smirk slinked across Chip's face, and his eyes narrowed as though he were peering at his target through a high-precision gunsight. "Wow! To be able to see all that you *say* you saw! Considering the known fact that, whatever happened, happened beyond the scope of the car lights. Considering the known fact that there was considerable cloud cover that night!" Chip had a knack for hammering home the information. "Boy, you must have really keen eyesight, that right?"

"Well, I . . . yes sir."

Then whipping a square of white paper from his vest pocket, Mr. Burwick waved it overhead like a flag before presenting it with a grand flourish to the now obviously weary and wilting witness. "For the sake of the jury would you kindly identify the paper that you are now holding?"

"You want me to read it out loud? What it says here?"

"I want you to tell me what you're holding. For what purpose, Miss Wayland, this was written."

She glanced down at the paper once more before looking up to face the smug, good looks of Roswell "Chip" Burwick, Esq. "Well, what this is is a prescription for eyeglasses written by Doctor John C. Taylor."

"Right! Exactly right!" exclaimed the counsel for the defense while clapping his hands together in an uncontrollable show of enthusiasm. "Now kindly read the name of the patient, the person for whom these glasses were prescribed."

Her head felt as though it were now going through the spin cycle. Why it couldn't be true—why, it wouldn't make a bit of sense for Mr. Burwick to make a big deal over the fact that sometimes when she had a lot of reading to do, she remembered to put on her glasses.

"Answer the question, Miss Wayland! For whom were these glasses intended?"

"Me."

Cupping his hand around his ear as though he had, within the last thirty seconds, grown deaf, Chip called out loudly, "Kindly repeat so I can hear your last statement. For whom were these glasses intended?"

"Me," she replied. "They were intended for me."

Then, as though coming from a great Greek chorus with perfect pitch as well as perfect timing, an oversized ensemble of, "HMMmmmm . . ." echoed throughout the room. Mr. Burwick, hands on hips, paused dramatically, allowing the jurors to digest that choice little morsel of information. But in the very next moment the stillness was shattered by his next question. "Miss Wayland, are you a popular girl?"

Carla stared in shocked disbelief at the questioner; her already moistureless mouth grew as parched as the Sahara. "Sir?"

Mr. Burwick allowed the barest beginning of a smile to play lightly across his lips. "The question was, Are *you* a popular girl?"

"I . . . I don't know."

"Oh, come on now, Miss Wayland," he chided, giving her a knowing wink. "It's such an easy question. Are you popular? How many boyfriends have you had before Andrew Harris?"

Carla's eyes sought out Mr. Wayne Dillman, the man whose side she was on. She was waiting for the prosecutor to shout out something helpful like "irrelevant," but she waited in vain.

"Please . . . just answer the question!"

Much of what Carla was feeling was revealed in her voice. With a dusty, dry-boned whisper, she responded, "I don't know."

"Answer the question!"

"I already told you—I don't know!"

"Allow me to help you out. Prior to Andy Harris, have you had more than ten boyfriends?"

"Ten boy friends? Uh, no sir."

"Well, how about eight?" chirped Chip, as though he were just now happily getting into the swing of things. "Have you had, say, more than eight boyfriends?"

Before seating herself in the witness stand, Carla had carefully instructed herself not to squirm. Is it possible, she wondered, that she had been squirming? "No sir, not that many."

"Six? As many as six?"

"Well . . . no, not six."

"Four?"

"Uh, no, I don't think—not four."

"Two?" Chip demanded, arching one of his shaped-like-a-comma eyebrows. "Have you had at least two?"

Slowly and sadly the girl shook her head no. It was as though even this small effort took too much, way too much effort. Then, shielding her eyes from scrutiny as though she were well on her way to becoming an object of public pity, she dropped her gaze downward as though all the answers demanded of her could best be found by examining all ten of her long and slender fingers. She sought out her mom and her friend Debby in the crowd—just looking at them would give her the courage she needed.

Gently, Chip Burwick caressed the knot of his designer necktie before addressing Judge Bernhardt. "If it pleases the court, Your Honor, allow the record to show that the witness has indicated by the negatively shaking of her head that she has had fewer than two boyfriends."

"So be it," intoned the judge. "Let the record so show."

"Miss Wayland, to be completely accurate—and I hope that you will agree with me that this jury which represents the public deserves no less—isn't it true that prior to Andy Harris you'd never had a boyfriend? That Andrew Harris was, in fact, the first and only boyfriend that you've ever had?"

How could Mr. Burwick ask that? To admit to that would make her enemies cheer and everyone else think of her as a total loser. A very public loser. Allowing herself what she rarely allowed herself—a furtive glance over at the defense table to momentarily gaze upon the guy who was once "her guy"—she could see that he was beginning to enjoy—no, he already *was* enjoying her discomfort. "Oh, no, sir," she heard herself respond. "Andy—he was not the first or only boyfriend that I've had."

Then as swiftly as a master magician's sleight-of-hand, the lawyer for the defense whipped from his suit jacket a folded sheet of pale pink paper. "Do you recognize this handwriting, Miss Wayland?" he demanded while thrusting the letter a few inches from her face.

Audibly Carla took in a lungful of air. "It looks like it might be . . . mine."

"Don't play games with me!" barked Chip. "Is it or is it not your handwriting?"

Although she continued to stare at the letter, it wasn't actually necessary to read its entire contents to realize not only who had written it, but also who had received it.

"Did you write this letter?"

"I . . ."

"Did YOU write this letter!?"

"I—yes! Yes, I wrote it."

"Read it!" commanded the counsel for the defense.

A peek over at Wayne Dillman to see if he was poised to object to this much too personal demand immediately showed Carla that he wasn't. As she focused on the words she had written, she felt the pain of having her privacy snatched from her. Clutching her throat as though that were going to help squeeze the words out, she began to read:

> Dearest darling Andy,
> All day and all night I dream of you.
> I can't imagine what I've done to deserve
> your love, but I'm so happy that I have your love.
> You will always Always ALWAYS have mine.
> You're my first love! My best love!
> My only love!
>
> I love you today, tomorrow, and forever!
> Carla

The girl looked up from the letter she had read to see Andy's attorney, hands dug deep into his pants pockets grinning at her discomfort. He twirled on the heels of his highly polished black shoes. "My first love . . . my best love," he mocked. "My *only* love. Please be advised, Miss Wayland, that lying to this court constitutes perjury, a punishable offense!"

Is that what she had done, Carla asked herself. Lied in this courtroom? Lied under oath? Lied merely to save herself from the humiliation of publicly admitting that never in her life had a boy liked her. Never until Andy Harris had a boy liked her!

Even as she felt Roswell "Chip" Burwick invade her

space, Carla Wayland still did not look up. "Miss Wayland, let's momentarily leave the numbers game. Please be good enough to tell this court what the following people have in common: Kimberly Ellen Watters, Jenny Lee Larsen, Sharon McAlister, Jennifer Masters, Bonnie Sue Andrews, and Karen Sue Benson?"

Lifting her eyes—even the effort of hoisting up her buttery brown eyes to face the counsel for the defense—added just that much extra energy to what was already bone-tired fatigue. "Girls . . . they're all girls I know."

The lawyer scoffed. "Oh, I bet you can do better than that. Specifically *who* are these girls?"

Carla took a deep breath. "Well, they've graduated Rachetville High School, everybody except Jenny Lee who is in the junior class with me."

"All right let's not play games, for instead of dancing with you"—Chip Burwick was moving closer and closer still to the witness stand—"you—the girl he brought to the prom—he danced with these girls? Isn't that so? Didn't he dance with them!?"

"Well, no—I mean—"

His face was now within striking distance of her face. "Did he dance with them?"

"Well . . . we—Andy and I both—"

"Answer the question: Did he dance with them?"

"I guess he . . ."

"Just answer the question: Did he dance with them?" His warm moist breath blasted heat against her face. "Dances he didn't dance with you, he danced with them?"

"Yes . . . yes."

"Miss Wayland, why don't you make a clean breast of it? Why don't you come right out and admit that if Andrew Harris had paid more attention to you and less attention to those other young ladies, you would not have gone to such lengths to punish him?"

"No!"

"And without the jealousy factor," continued Mr. Burwick without any noticeable pause, "there would have been no trial because there was foolishness, YES! There was recklessness, YES! There was an accident, YES! There was a tragedy, YES! But there was NO malice, NO premeditation, and certainly there was NO crime!"

Chapter 22

THE TRIAL OF the Rachetville Five ended dramatically on October 9 at 11:35 in the morning when the foreman of the jury, Horace Morris, cleared the phlegm from his throat before announcing the verdict: "involuntary manslaughter."

Relief and happiness exploded throughout the courtroom as the young defendants hugged, kissed, and cheered. Repeatedly jabbing the air with his right fist, Andy yelled to nobody in particular, but to everybody in general, "We did it! We *did* it!" Almost immediately Chip Burwick's cheeks were imprinted, although not necessarily improved by, multiple lip-prints from Elna Jean Harris.

There was so much commotion in the mahogany-walled courtroom that the judge had trouble restoring order long enough to announce that sentencing would take place six weeks hence, at ten o'clock in the morning on November 16.

OUTSIDE THE WAYLAND home on the November morning of the sentencing, the Japanese maple tree had already lost some of its leaves, and the real estate broker's sign in front of the house proclaimed to friends and foes alike that there was a sale pending.

Judith knocked lightly on the door of her daughter's bedroom. "We don't have a lot of time. Ready for breakfast?"

Carla swung open the door. She wore a baby-blue skirt and a matching sweater, and around her neck was a single very ladylike strand of cultured pearls. "Fooled you, didn't I?"

Judith beamed, relieved to see Carla was on the mend. A person who's young and healthy could accomplish an awful lot of healing in forty-two days—thank God! Carla had left the court at the trial's end with one profusely bleeding wound that no emergency medical personnel could ever treat because the trauma had been to her mind . . . and to her spirit.

As Judith closely observed her daughter, she silently asked herself the same old nagging question that had clung to her like a chronic headache for six weeks. Why should the young person who suffered the most from the trial and its aftermath be Carla and not one of those five charged with murder? Why was it the one, the only one, fired up with a passion for justice?

Justice? In spite of herself, the mere thought of that word made the librarian shake her head mournfully. Justice . . . the community didn't want it, the jurors didn't dispense it, and Lord knows, the lawyers seemed to have the least regard for it. Why, Judith pondered, were attorneys forever referring to themselves as "practicing law"? Why wouldn't they come right out and call it by its rightful name: practicing the *avoidance* of law?

But if there was pain, and there *was* pain aplenty, it was also true that not everything was sorrow and loss, loss and sorrow.

There was also pride. The shared pride of a mother and daughter who grew closer in the knowledge that they may have been knocked around but they had never been knocked out. For Judith, there was the exhilaration of being able to gaze on her own child and say with complete candor, "You're okay, kiddo. I'm proud of you."

If there was any one thing that had crystallized this point of honor between them, it was Carla herself, who came to the difficult decision that whatever the price, she had to give testimony to the truth, the whole truth, and nothing but the truth. The truth exactly as she had experienced it.

At the breakfast table, Judith split the four-egg mushroom omelet that Carla had cooked to perfection as they chatted about the weather. Carla considered that a form of talking without saying anything but, ever since the trial, that kind of talk had pretty much suited her.

Judith looked out the kitchen window in time to see the brittle fallen leaves being pushed into a dancing frenzy. "It's a cinch we won't be needing our lawn mower until spring," she said. "Think we should get it tuned up before taking it with us?"

"If you're bent on taking that temperamental old gas mower with us to Peterborough, then why bother to ask my opinion?"

"Because I value it."

Carla sighed. "I sure wish others still did."

"Don't tell me—is that regret I'm hearing? Are you sorry that you testified to the truth?"

"No, but I wish . . . well, I guess I wish that truth didn't hurt so much," she responded with a quick toss of her head.

Judith laughed. "And so, my darling, do I."

"Going back into that courtroom today to hear Judge Bernhardt pass sentence . . . I feel funny about that." Carla speared an escaped mushroom cap with her fork, without bothering to eat it. "Will people—Andy and the others—think I'm only there to gloat? Because I'm the only one not charged with the crime? Is that what they'll think?"

Slowly Judith thinly spread low-salt, low-fat, low-taste margarine on her whole-wheat toast. "Try not to worry about them anymore, honey. It's not really rewarding trying to fathom what people will think. Particularly people who have demonstrated a lifetime aversion to thinking. What is important to remember is why you decided to testify in spite of everything. Right from the start you realized that some people would consider you a traitor. But in spite of everything you decided to forge ahead. It had a lot to do with facing yourself, remember?"

Carla's low chuckle could have easily been mistaken for a moan. "I still can't get over how Andy's lawyer tried to make me tell the court that I ran away from the others that night because of jealousy. He pretended that it had nothing at all to do with the fact that I feared Stephan might be in jeopardy." She shook her head in disbelief. "Waking up the Lindstrom family at one in the morning and begging them to call the Parson Springs police was just what any normal girl would do if her boyfriend wasn't giving her enough attention.

Right? Well some people—probably a lot of people— believe that! They really believe that I was trying to punish Andy! And, oh yes, the fact that a man really did drown was just one of those things. Nothing but a real peculiar kind of a coincidence."

"I'm sorry that I have to agree with you, because unfortunately Mr. Burwick did perform altogether competently. He did what he was paid to do. In painting you as a girl burning with jealousy over Andy's romantic interest in others, he made all your testimony suspect."

Thoughtfully, Carla replaced the top on the jar of marmalade. "I know. It's called discrediting the witness."

Judith decisively pushed her plate toward the center of the table. "In the end the jury believed you! The Rachetville Five *were* convicted."

"Convicted yes, but convicted of murder? No! They were convicted only of involuntary manslaughter!" Carla shook her head as though she were trying to shake away some terrible but persistent truth. "Take away all the legal mumbo jumbo and all that means is that no malice was ever intended, only that these 'nice, young people' should have been more careful. Want to know something, Mom? When I worked at the day-care center that's just what they paid me to say to the children when they spilled their milk: 'Oh, I know it was an accident,' I'd tell them, 'Only next time, let's see how we can be more careful.' "

At Carla's flash of insight, Judith laughed approvingly, and it was just the warmth emanating from her mother's compassion that propelled her to open up in a way that she hadn't since the trial.

"Want to know what else made me furious?"

Judith looked up at Carla, who narrowed her eyes and continued, gesticulating with her hands and aping Burwick. " 'Forgive this girl,' he told the jurors, ' 'cause it's not her fault, 'cause she never asked to be born to a dangerously radical mother.' "

Judith replied, "No doubt about it, we took our licks all right. What he said about me should have been stricken but the case wasn't really fair from many points of view. However, in the end the jury did convict them."

"Only of involuntary manslaughter," shot back Carla. "Don't you see, Mother . . . don't you see, *I* was guilty of involuntary manslaughter—they were guilty of *murder*!"

Judith jumped to her feet. "*You* were guilty of *nothing*! You tried to save Stephan Jones! Remember that you, and only you, tried to save—"

Carla interrupted. "That night I tried . . . I *really* tried to save him. . . ." She bit down on her lower lip so that the physical pain could divert her attention from the emotional pain of remembering. Her eyes were touched by mist. "But tell me," she went on, "where was I when all those ugly homophobic jokes were being told? The truth is I was standing right there with the others laughing my head off. Where was I when Andy harassed Stephan and Frank with letters, phone calls, and vandalism? I'm so ashamed because I kept looking up in Andy's eyes and telling him how wonderful he really was! I keep thinking and wondering, would things have turned out differently if I had been different? If right from the beginning I had demanded that Andy leave those men alone?"

Judith rubbed two fingers back and forth across her forehead as though anticipating a headache. "None of us can fly backwards in time to correct our wrongs of yesterday," she said. "So perhaps, the next best thing is to have the courage to face those past wrongs. By confronting them we change ourselves! Somewhere within yourself you discovered that kind of courage. I admire you for it."

The phone jangled, breaking the mood, and both women looked anxiously at each other before responding to its ring. While reaching for it, Judith shook her head in exasperation. "When you have to think twice about the wisdom of answering your own phone, then it's really time to move on." But on the line was Debby's mother, Peg Packard. She and Debby wanted to accompany them to court. Since Carla was close enough to hear Peg's question, all Judith had to do was to lift a quizzical eyebrow in her daughter's direction and wait a mere fraction of a beat as Carla smiled and nodded affirmatively.

Chapter 23

ACROSS THE WINDING Pascaloosa River over in Parson Springs, the rising November sun peeked around and through the calico curtains of the graceful home that Frank Montgomery once shared with Stephan Jones.

Frank stood in front of his bathroom sink, shaving. Today this ordinary, everyday ritual felt different. Perhaps it was merely the intensity with which he glared back at his reflection that made it more than clear that this was no ordinary day.

Hanging from a hanger on the bathroom door was a carefully laid-out business suit with an accompanying no-nonsense striped tie and a white oxford cloth shirt.

As he shaved, he heard a familiar thud against his door. Without bothering to wipe the shaving cream from his face, he walked briskly out his front door to pick up his weekly copy of the *Parson Springs Transcript* lying on the sun-shaded veranda. He stood outside in the morning light totally engrossed in the lead article: RACHETVILLE FIVE TO BE SENTENCED TODAY: CONVICTED LAST MONTH OF INVOLUNTARY MANSLAUGHTER.

Returning inside, he tossed away the second section and placed the first section on his dining room table where he carefully constructed two folds. Then he bound both ends with pieces of surgical tape, creating a kind of pocket with an opening only from the top.

From outside he suddenly heard a chorus of raucous young voices shouting, "Frank-Frank! Frank Montgomery! Frank-Frank! Frank Montgomery!" Swinging open the front door, he was bombarded by an assault of screaming obscenities hurled at him from the safety of a nearly new Oldsmobile.

With fists raised, Frank dashed after the now quickly accelerating automobile, shouting at full volume, "For what you did, you'll pay! If it's the last thing I ever do, you'll pay! I swear to God YOU'LL PAY!!!"

Alone, Frank Montgomery drove the Winnebago to Rachetville. As he passed the courthouse, a cameraman, sporting the NBC peacock on his equipment, was setting up in a particularly strategic spot. The block was jammed with cameramen and reporters from local as well as national press and TV stations. Overnight entrepreneurs with houses within a few blocks of the courthouse were renting out their driveways, and even their yards, for three bucks a clip.

Some blocks away on a side street Frank pulled his RV over to the edge of the curb and cut the motor. Next to him on the passenger's seat was his copy of the *Transcript* with its specially prepared pocket. It didn't lie flat as before. There was something inside that was giving it a hefty bulge.

Walking across the courthouse lawn with the newspaper pressed tight beneath his arm, Frank Montgomery passed beneath the shadow of a bronze Confederate soldier. Although seven generations separated the soldier from the antique dealer, it was clear they shared something. Maybe it was only the rage of men who had seen the unbelievable and experienced the unspeakable.

A few steps later, Frank stopped short to take in the sweet aroma wafting from several pushed-together card tables laden with home-baked cakes, pies, and cookies. The sugar and cinnamon fragrance momentarily transported Frank back through time and space to the days he'd been wrapped in his grandmother's loving embrace before being led into her sugar-and-spice kitchen.

He smiled wanly and noticed on the card table his absolute favorite: moist chocolate brownie squares topped with chunky bits of walnuts. Frank took out his wallet while asking one of the pleasant-looking ladies behind the table, "How much for the brownie?"

"Anything you'd like to contribute *over* a dollar, sir," she sang out sweetly. "It's all for a good cause, you know."

For the first time, Frank noticed the poster-board sign written somewhat crudely in red and green Magic Markers and stuck with Scotch tape to the edge of the card table: Buy a Pie and sweeten the defense fund of the Rachetville Five . . . Sponsored by The Ladies Auxiliary of The Rachetville Baptist Church.

"How much would you like to contribute, sir?" she asked, her deep Southern accent carrying as much of a sugary glaze as her bakery goods.

In contrast, it made Frank's response sound just that

much more rude: "Nothing!" he spit out, as he whipped his unopened wallet back into his back pocket. "Not a damn thing!"

As he approached the courthouse, he wondered if in the fifty years since the Scopes trial, had so many out-of-town media types descended upon such a sleepy Southern town.

Striding energetically toward Frank was a beefy man in his late thirties whom everybody called "Red" all the years he was growing up in Fitzgerald, Georgia. "Red" in more recent years had changed his three-letter nickname back to the three-letter name he had been given at birth: Ben.

Hereabouts, Ben Brewster was mockingly referred to as "the First Fag" because he was sent by the National Gay and Lesbian Task Force all the way from Washington, D.C., to organize local protests as well as to monitor the trial. As he fell into step with Frank Montgomery, an anxious look played across his face. "How are you today, Frank? Are you okay?" he queried. "Anything that either I or the task force can do to help?"

"The only thing I care about is justice," Frank answered grimly. "I must see those animals given some kind of punishment—there's got to be something that, at the very least, acknowledges that a crime has been committed."

"From your lips to God's ears," answered Ben, trying for a slightly lighter note. "I guess that's what we'd all like to—"

Frank gestured dramatically with his right hand while his left arm squeezed the bulging newspaper even closer to his body. "You didn't hear me, Ben! I didn't say that the punishment of Andrew Harris and company would be *nice* or desirable or something pleasant to contemplate. What I said was I *must* see punishment. MUST! Must see punishment!"

"And he *will* be punished, too," Ben said soothingly, dropping a fraternal arm over Frank's shoulder. "That's what the sentencing is all about. Believe me, I know what you're feeling."

Frank halted in mid-stride. "You haven't a clue," he lambasted the gay rights organizer. "Not unless you happen to know what it feels like to walk around without skin. I feel as though I've had all my skin peeled away. Ever since I saw what those people did to Stevie, I've felt skinless and without protective covering, everything about me is exposed. And everything hurts like hell."

"Seeing the Rachetville Five punished," Ben started, "will go some distance in helping you heal I suppose?"

"Yes, yes . . . that and . . ."

"And what?"

Frank looked down. "It sounds so selfish. What with Stevie's life finished before he could finish living it . . ."

"But Stevie's not in pain anymore," Ben interjected with exquisite understanding. "You are. I'd honestly like to know if there's anything—anything at all we can do to help you?"

"What I'd like more than anything else," Frank said, finally allowing his eyes to connect with Ben's, "is for somebody in the straight community to express sympathy." He shook his head as though he, of all people, were at an absolute loss to understand this need of his, much less explain it. "Why is it . . . I mean why can't they realize that there's no such thing as gay grief or straight grief? Why can't they understand that grief comes completely without gender, without affectional preference? It offers an absolutely nonracist, nonsexist, nonbigoted, nonhomophobic equal opportunity employment to all!"

Ben smiled wanly. "Some straight people here and there already understand that. Maybe someday they all will."

Frank Montgomery looked off into the faraway distance. "Until then I'll probably keep on fantasizing that somebody—my landlord, mechanic, neighbor—somebody will drop an arm around my shoulder or maybe just touch my hand and say, 'Frank, I was real sorry to learn that you lost your friend.' What makes it so impossibly difficult for one human being to reach out to another? To say something as simple and as wonderful as that. Isn't it strange," he asked, pausing long enough to mentally frame the question, "that not one person can even bring themselves to say that?"

Ben's response was totally drowned out by the wild cheering of young people's voices, mostly female. They were loudly screaming:

> Andy . . . Andy . . . He's our man!
> Andy . . . Andy . . . He's our man!
> Andy . . . Andy . . . He's our man!
> He can do what nobody can!
> Hooray Andy! Hooray Harris!
> Hooray ANDY HARRIS!! HOORAY!!!

As the young man who was the center of all the attention and admiration stepped from his father's Oldsmobile, he flashed his cheerleaders a confident grin as well as ironically the exact same "V for Victory" sign that the victorious American general once flashed to a grateful world at the very moment that Nazi Germany begged for peace. Following their young hero out of the car was his fashionably dressed mother, his grim-faced father, his thin-lipped lawyer, and their freshly coiffed minister, Reverend Roland B. Wheelwright.

The media pressed tight around Andy's group shooting questions: "Are you nervous? Andy, are you confident? Any regrets that you'd like to express to Stephan Jones's survivors, Loretta and Lloyd Jones or Frank Montgomery? Any guilt over what happened? In your opinion did the jury last month treat the Rachetville Five fairly when they found you guilty of manslaughter?"

Attorney Chip Burwick shepherded his young client through the maze, all the time repeating: "Andrew Harris will have absolutely no comment at this time. I'm sorry, ladies and gentlemen, but Andrew Harris will have no comment to make at this time."

As the others skipped up the courthouse steps, the Reverend Wheelwright lingered behind to answer a question put to him by a pretty television reporter whose face as well as name was well known to viewers of the ABC affiliate station in Fayetteville. Her question to the preacher was lost in the din, but in a live feed to the local station, the clergyman's face as well as his response was heard by thousands: ". . . After all, it was Jones's aggressive homosexual behavior that precipitated his death." He smiled a smile that would do credit to a saint. "Why, if only Stephan Jones hadn't made sexual advances toward a red-blooded, *real* boy like Andrew Harris, then he'd be walking the streets of Parson Springs today. No doubt about it!"

Back at the station in the living room setting of the morning show, the silver-haired cohost, Billy Barnard, raised his eyebrows before turning to his TV partner, Sherry Lee West. "If you did in every man who made a pass at you, Sherry Lee, I bet the male population of Fayetteville would be a heck of a lot thinner. Right?"

Chapter 24

PEG PACKARD PULLED her fading blue Toyota directly in front of the courthouse square so that Carla, Judith, and Debby could make a quick entrance into the building before the media knew what was what. But before they made it inside the dignified old edifice, the cry went up, "There's Carla!" One or two alert photographers were able to capture a picture.

As the women raced inside the protective doors, the photographers and reporters turned to recording the two distinct groups of demonstrators that were springing into action. Women, mostly thick-set and middle-aged, were waving high the banner of the Christian Decency League. Across the lawn the National Gay and Lesbian Task Force was out waving their signs. The task force crowd was about half the age of the CDL.

If there was, however, any single attribute that was shared by both the league and the task force, besides the not-so-obvious fact that they all belonged to the human race, it was that both groups were convinced beyond any quibble or question that God, honor, beauty, and all things noble resided totally and solely within the confines of their own position.

Ben Brewster had given out preprinted placards as well as black balloons with pink triangles. "Now whatever happens remember this: No matter what the provocation, you must exert, at all times, Gandhi-like self-discipline."

"What if they call us faggots?" shot back a college-age fellow. "Can't we, at least, call them breeders?"

"You certainly cannot!" retorted Ben, scorching the questioner with a searing look. "That's sexist . . . offensive to *all* women! Offensive to everybody! For God sakes, Warren, responding to hate *with* hate brings us down to *their* level. We must never do that—we don't have to—we have morality on our side."

As the members of the task force began their orderly albeit enthusiastic trek around the courthouse square, Ben initiated a chant: "Hay-Hay . . . Ho-Ho . . . Homophobia has got to go! Hay-Hay . . . Ho-Ho . . . Homophobia has got to go! Hay-Hay . . . Ho-Ho . . . Homophobia has got to go!" And as they marched and chanted, they bobbed their helium balloons skyward and waved their placards:

THE RELIGIOUS RIGHT IS NEITHER!
HOMOPHOBIA IS A SOCIAL DISEASE
I BELIEVE IN FAIRIES
DIGNITY/LITTLE ROCK
THOU SHALT NOT KILL
WE ARE AN ANGRY GENTLE PEOPLE
FREEDOM AND JUSTICE FOR ALL
HETEROSEXUAL ALLY
STEPHAN JONES DIED FOR YOUR SINS

WE ARE YOUR CHILDREN
MOTHER OF A PROUD GAY SON
IS ANDREW HARRIS A HERO FOR KILLING A MAN?
IS STEPHAN JONES A VILLAIN FOR LOVING A MAN?

And trotting alongside the ankles of one of the lead marchers were two miniature dachshunds sporting pink bow ties, and dangling just beneath each of the well-cared-for pets' necks was a neatly penned sign proclaiming I'M ONE, TOO.

As the colorful, chanting, waving members of the task force marched past the sedate members of the CDL, even the air molecules between the two sides felt as though they had become hypercharged with electricity. On signal from their leader, Virginia Foley, the entire contingent from the Christian Decency League placed their hands over their hearts and began to proudly sing, "God Bless America." But as soon as the last note had finished resonating in the morning air, Virginia boomed out, "Everybody ready? Raise your banners!" With a restrained cheer, a profusion of CDL placards were proudly hoisted high:

GOD LOVES THE SINNER BUT HATES THE SIN
PRAY FOR THE RACHETVILLE FIVE
IF HOMOSEXUALS POPULATED THE EARTH,
THERE WOULD BE NO POPULATION
YOU CAN CHANGE
GOD MADE ADAM AND EVE. NOT ADAM AND STEVE!
DO AWAY WITH AIDS. STAMP OUT HOMOSEXUALITY
HOMOSEXUALITY . . . CAN BE OVERCOME!
REPENT
EXODUS INTERNATIONAL
HOMOSEXUALITY IS AN ABOMINATION
READ YOUR BIBLE
THE WAGES OF SIN IS DEATH

Although court had not yet been called to order, the standing-room-only assembly bustled and buzzed with intense energy. Carla, sitting rigidly between her mother and Debby, struggled to control her nervousness. Would the sentencing of her five former friends at long last settle things? At least in her own mind?

Although sentencing was not scheduled until ten o'clock, the courtroom had been packed to capacity since nine. Carla glanced at her watch for the fifth time in the last four minutes and wondered if the minute hand would ever advance beyond six.

Closing her eyes, she listened as outdoors on the village green, the voices of the Christian Decency League sang with haunting harmony. "Onward Christian soldiers . . . Marching as to war . . . with the cross of Jesus . . . going on before. . . ."

When she opened her eyes next, she caught sight of Andy seating himself next to his lawyer at the defendants' table, and she thought: Yes, he did look good, as good as he had ever looked. But the big difference now was that she no longer felt physically drawn to those looks, no matter how objectively handsome. Oh sure, he was still a very pretty package all right with nothing but hate and hollowness inside.

Her first sweet sweep of emotion over Andy Harris and over belonging to his perfect family seemed so very long ago and far away. Back then, she would have sworn on the graves of her ancestors that what she felt was love. Love, pure and simple. Love sweet love, love forever, love. The next time she called herself "in love," she would make completely sure that she loved not just the surface stuff she could see, but the deeper, more real qualities, those qualities which the eyes alone could never penetrate.

Rising majestically above the crowded room's din was a single voice of commanding authority. "Hear ye . . . Hear ye . . . All rise and give your attention and draw nigh," intoned the blue uniformed bailiff. His voice snapped Carla out of her reveries and back to the present. "The honorable Morris Bernhardt, presiding Judge.

Following Andy in a neat, somber line before the bar of justice were Mike, Doug, Lisa, and Donna. Judge Bernhardt strode to the bench without seeming to take any particular notice of his jammed-to-capacity courtroom. Papers were passed to the judge for signing. Finally he cleared his throat, peered over a pair of half-glasses, and asked the defendants to face the bench for sentencing. As soon as he made that statement, the whole room became quieter and stiller than a mausoleum at midnight.

For what felt like a long period of time, the judge stared at the scrubbed and shiny young people who forty-two days earlier had been convicted of involuntary manslaughter. He put his hands deep into the folds of his black robe as he made *tsk-tsk-tsk*ing sounds with the tip of his tongue. "Now, boys—and young ladies, too—what you all have done is something you ought not be proud of. Since this jury has found you guilty of involuntary manslaughter in the death of Stephan Jones, it becomes my grave duty as the judge to pronounce sentence.

"I believe what you all did was more of a result of your young age than of any ill will or maliciousness. Furthermore, I do not for an instant believe that your young lives, or our society, for that matter, will be improved one iota by sentencing you five young people to Tucker Prison Farm. I could surely do so, and you could spend the next five years learning how to be *real* criminals."

The very fabric of Andy's trousers was trembling as he stood pale and wan before the judge who looked as though he had, at least momentarily, run out of things to say. But just as Carla and the other spectators began wondering if that was all, Judge Bernhardt started speaking again. "I have decided to sentence you all— each and every one of you—to one year in prison."

A group gasp of disbelief was echoed throughout the courtroom. "But . . ." continued the magistrate, holding one stern finger aloft, even as the sound of that anguished gasp continued to resonate, "I will suspend that sentence on the condition that you all properly participate in our parole program, and that individually you do at least one hundred hours of community service."

Judge Bernhardt lifted his black-robed arm to give a mighty whack of his mahogany gavel. "This court stands adjourned," he declared as he stood up. From somewhere toward the back of the room, a single "Yippee!!" erupted. People jumped to their feet stomping, shouting, and applauding, loudly applauding. Then from nowhere and everywhere there were people, people rushing to touch, hold, hug, and sometimes kiss all the members of the Rachetville Five.

Judith reached out to squeeze Carla's hand. "It's not the five people who took Stephan Jones's life that should be applauded. It's you and Frank Montgomery, the two people who tried to *save* his life!"

With a notable lack of energy, Carla nodded and weakly smiled back. Judith said, "Well, I guess that's that," trying to sound more matter-of-fact than she felt. "Let's get out of here."

Peg and Debby Packard hugged Carla and without any further comment began threading their way through the melee of rejoicing celebrants. As they approached the front steps of the courthouse, Carla turned to her mother as Judith attempted to steer her down the concrete steps. "Mother, I can't leave just yet. There's something I have to do."

"What?"

"Well, I'm not . . . exactly sure."

"I'm not in any hurry," Judith said as she turned to Peg Packard. "Are you?"

"Mother, please . . . I'd really prefer it if the three of you just went on. I'll get home."

Judith's worried look returned, flicking across her brow, but Carla interrupted before her mother had time to form her worries into words. "I'll be fine— please, Mom, we'll talk when I get home. I promise I won't be long."

Judith nodded reluctantly. Debby threw her best friend a puzzled look but simply said, "I'll call you later, Carla, or you call me. Okay?"

"Thanks, Debby."

As Carla watched the three women negotiate their way down the courthouse steps, she made her way to a spot at the far edge of the building where she observed the exiting throng. She knew that she had to stay at this scene, although she didn't know why. She had an uneasy feeling that something wasn't finished. Something still needed doing. But exactly what needed doing, she didn't know.

An exuberant Andy Harris, sandwiched between his grinning lawyer and his thrilled mother, swept out of the building and into the warm and welcoming glow of sunlight. But just before starting down the stairway,

Andy stopped when he saw Carla. He caught and held her eyes.

She felt a range of emotions; chief among them was amazement that she could now look upon a person she once thought she loved and feel only disgust. Another emotion that filled her was sadness, as real and thick as London fog. Sadness that a sweet and gentle man lay in his grave, and in her own hometown, people who ought to know better acclaimed and applauded his murderers.

Carla's face exposed her complex web of feelings, but then Andy's face wasn't exactly keeping government secrets. His lower lip curled under while his left eyebrow arched. So what registered there was pure industrial-strength contempt. Rapidly, he scanned his repertory of insults for an ego-crushing zinger to finally put Carla in her place for all time. He called out across the crowd, "Hey Carla Wayland, I heard you and your mother are moving to New Hampshire. Just don't think you'll be any more popular there than you are here. Everyone will find out about you and how you're a rat fink!"

He waited for a response that wasn't forthcoming, as she stared at him in amazement. Much the way she'd stare at someone who was growing smaller and smaller before her very eyes. Then Andrew Anthony Harris snapped his head and his attention away from Carla to go skipping lightly down the steps of justice, where his friends and neighbors waited expectantly, along with happy relatives, some who had traveled here all the way from Jonesboro, Tyronza, and Parkin.

As the girl watched him move with manly grace to mix and mingle on the green with the still-gathering throng, she wondered, Was that the end? All there was to it? Had she made herself stick around for nothing more important than to see Andy for one final time and to be the recipient of his insult? Was everything all tied up and finished? She felt drained all the way down to empty.

Spotting a hub of activity near the statue of the Confederate soldier, Carla observed the subdued and haunted looks of the members of the Gay and Lesbian Task Force. Several women and at least one man were openly crying. At first, she wondered why the entire group huddled together, and then she thought she understood. Being close might provide them with a touch of warmth in an otherwise cold and cruel world.

As Carla wandered near this cheerless, crowded group, she noticed a young woman with carrot-colored hair. Tears were streaming down her cheeks as she cried out to nobody in particular and to anybody and everybody who would listen: "If there's no punishment for killing one of us, then doesn't that mean that in the eyes of the law we're not human? Not really human?"

Chapter 25

YARDS DISTANT FROM the members of the task force was the distraught Frank Montgomery with his hands thrust deep within his pockets. A fat copy of the local newspaper was still jammed against his body. Without knowing exactly why or what she planned to do, once she arrived there, Carla found herself walking over to Frank. When he saw that it was her, he looked up and said, "Hello."

"Hello," she answered back. As she stood facing him, her heart felt full of things that needed saying. And although time was passing without any more words spoken, strangely enough she didn't feel ill at ease. Even so, she didn't exactly know how to go picking and choosing amid all those pulls and tugs from her heartstrings. She did understand that standing here with this man was the only right and proper place to be. "I wrote you a letter, Frank. It was the day after it happened, after Stephan drowned."

"Strange I never received it."

"Not so strange, considering I never mailed it."

"Well, why not?" he asked, managing to sound at first pleased and then disappointed.

"For starters, I didn't know—I wasn't sure you'd want to hear from me."

"Oh, how I would have loved hearing from you!" The animation in Frank's face was more than matched by the animation in his voice. "What did you say?"

"I do remember that it was such a hard letter to write. . . . I kept trying to express what I felt, but the words—I could never find the words, certainly not the right words!"

"Then tell me now," said Frank, probing her eyes with his. "What was in your heart?"

"How terrible I felt about Stephan's drowning. I wrote you that I hurt for you losing a loved one. I know nothing hurts like that hurts . . . nothing!" Then when Carla saw that her words were bringing tears to his eyes, she instinctively reached out to take his hand. "I'm sorry. Honestly, I didn't mean to bring you more pain than you already have."

"You didn't!" he corrected, smiling in spite of the tear he quickly captured as it raced down his cheekbone. "You have only brought me pleasure. I'm sorry to hear you have also lost a loved one."

"Hmmm . . . maybe *lost* isn't exactly the right word because I'm not sure that you can lose what you've never had. I've never known my dad, but that doesn't stop me from missing him."

Frank bent his head to kiss her hand. "You're special," he told her. "A very special lady."

He smiled at her with a smile that was at the same time unspeakably sad and unquestionably honest. She responded by squeezing his hand in unspoken gratitude. It made her remember what she felt when first he whispered to her on that December night in front of Harris's Handy Hardware Store. At that moment, like this moment, as well as like all those moments in between, she felt without question or quibble that Frank Montgomery was her friend.

Then in the next moment they were saying good-bye. And for some reason she didn't even dimly understand, Carla never moved from the spot where she stood. Frank smiled at her and turned. She continued to stand watching him as he strode with what seemed like clear determination past the tearful, yet still defiant members of the task force.

As Frank charged past, Ben Brewster glanced up. It was quick, but still and all, it was enough to tell him almost instantly that something wasn't right. While Andy Harris may have relaxed perceptibly since the sentencing, the same couldn't be said for Frank Montgomery. The vein at Frank's right temple was pulsating off and on like a neon sign. He was wound up as tightly as any coil that at any moment must *snap*!

Both Ben Brewster and Carla were staring in breathless anxiety as Frank marched in an unbroken line toward the winners' celebration circle. Inside this triumphant gathering of laughing friends, grinning lawyers, cheering families, and ever-curious reporters, Andrew Harris was turning into an instant media star. Even from Carla's fifty-foot distance, she could tell by his body language that he was answering even the difficult questions thrown at him with surprising poise and swift repartee.

Someone just happening on the scene would almost swear that this handsome and assured young man had certainly been recognized for some sort of significant achievement: winning a scholarship, hitting a home run, saving a child from being run over by a speeding car, or at the very least saving a pet from being run over by a speeding car.

As Frank marched closer to his target, his shoulders were suddenly grabbed from behind by the full-bodied arms of Ben Brewster. As he swung him around, Ben pleaded, "What do you think you're going to do, Frank? Stay away from that guy! You know—now, you know—that you don't need that kind of trouble! It's not going to bring Stephan back! It's not!"

"No, it won't bring Stevie back, but as you so correctly observed earlier, maybe I need something, too. And what I need, every bit as much as I need water to drink or air to breathe, is retribution. One way or another, I will see to it that Andy Harris is punished. He must be punished!"

Ben's hands went out in a desperate pleading gesture. "Don't, I beg of you, rush into doing something that for the rest of your life you'll regret. Wait until your grief is better under control! Wait until—"

Frank laughed, but it wasn't so much a laugh as it was a mock. "Why is it that your advice never changes, huh, Ben? At the beginning, you told me to wait, give it some time, and allow public opinion to turn against the Rachetville Five. But good ol' public opinion never did. Did it? Later you advised me to stay calm and wait for the jury's findings. Remember saying that, Ben? Still later, after they came back with involuntary manslaughter, your advice was not to do anything rash, but to wait for the sentencing. I did that, too, didn't I, Ben? Even so, it all came to the same thing. Zilch! Zero! So what good did all my waiting do? No good! No good at all. Wait! Wait! That's always been your answer, Ben! Well, I'm tired of waiting! I'm tired of your wimpish task force, and if the truth be known, I'm also tired of you!"

Then with a quarterback's maneuver that was as quick and agile as it was unexpected, Frank faked to the right while passing Ben on the left. Frank rushed over to where Andy and the other four members of the Rachetville Five were exuberantly bantering with each other, their relatives, friends, and more than a dozen members of the press.

It was in front of this astonished gathering that Frank Montgomery made a serene, but altogether conspicuous entrance.

"What the—" snarled Lawrence Harris. "Get the fuck out of here!"

"As you can plainly see, this *is* a private gathering," added Mrs. Harris, using her haughtiest tone. "For only close friends and well-wishers."

"Well, since those are your criteria," responded Frank, looking and sounding completely pleasant, "then you will have to admit, Mrs. Harris, that nobody could ever wish your son warmer wishes than I do."

Lawrence Harris made a get-out-of-here gesture with his thumb. "Move it, faggot! You're crazier than I thought! Don't make a scene in front of the TV or I'll . . ."

"Please . . . I'm not here to cause trouble for you or your family, Mr. Harris," Frank pleaded while shifting the bulging newspaper from beneath his left arm into his right hand. "For God's sake, Andy, the trial, the sentencing—it's all over with. You're safe now, nothing at all to be afraid of anymore."

"What is this anyway?" Andy Harris made a grinding noise, a little like a small engine badly in need of a tune-up. "What are you talking about?! Didn't you hear my daddy? Beat it, faggot!"

Taking no apparent notice of the taunt, Frank continued to show an altogether cheerful demeanor while making motions with his hands as though patting down air. "Hey, hey, big guy," he soothed as he glanced slyly to his right and left before finally focusing on the three Harrises. "I made you all a promise. Remember?" Although Frank spoke in a voice that mimicked a whisper, it still was strong enough to capture the attention of more and more members of the group. Ironman, Spider, and the girls all had heads sharply bent toward the speaker. And to the extent that the in-group had been, only two or three or four minutes ago, happily noisy, it had now become the absolute total opposite: quiet, oh so ungodly quiet.

Everywhere people turned to look and they seemed almost reluctant to breathe, fearing that the sounds coming from merely inhaling and exhaling would in some way interfere with their ability to hear Frank Montgomery . . . and to hear it all!

It was true that everybody was listening, but it was also true that only one person, only Andy, was the object of Frank's complete and total concentration. "I did what I told you I'd do! I kept my promise of silence throughout the entire ordeal, didn't I? If I didn't desert you then, why would I blow your cover now?"

Andy Harris turned toward his family and friends with outstretched palms. "I don't know what this guy is talking about! He must be crazy. I *swear* to God he's crazy!"

Mrs. Harris implored the intruder, "Please, please just go and join *your* kind!"

With all the flair of a master magician, Frank Montgomery waved before his audience's unblinking eyes a strangely misshapen edition of the *Parson Springs Transcript*. "I am now prepared to prove, Andy," announced Frank, pausing only long enough to allow the drama to build, "that my word is true!"

"Honestly, Mr. Montgomery," exclaimed Elna Harris through pinched lips, "don't you realize that you're upsetting us?"

Like a gentleman from another distant, more gentle, time, Frank acknowledged the lady's complaint with an elaborate and apologetic nod of his head. But then, abruptly shifting gears, Frank allowed his laserlike focus to return to Andy, as he announced grandly, "I *have* kept my promise. It's here and it's all for you." Reaching into the secret pocket within the paper, he whipped forth a packet of bluish-gray envelopes, all held together with a delicate and prettily tied blue ribbon.

"I don't know what you're talking about!" whined Andy. "Nobody here knows what you're talking about! So, fuck off, fag!"

"Now . . . now . . ." Frank responded by telegraphing a conspiratorial smile directly to Andy. "You know how I hate it when you go getting yourself all worked up. By the way, what you testified to about Stephan pestering you for sex . . . boy, could I have ever backed that up."

"No!" shrieked Andy. "You know it's not true—it never happened! It's only what Mr. Burwick told me to say!"

"Hey, relax," Frank ordered in his most tranquilizing tone. "I could never be mad at you, Andy. Stephan himself told me that after you guys had sex, you lost interest in him. That you only wanted me."

"What is this, some kind of joke?" Andy squealed. He giggled nervously as though there were some scheme afoot that he'd be catching on to at any second now. "If this is your idea of a joke, then it's not funny 'cause nobody's laughing, right gang?" He checked out the faces of his father, mother, Ironman, Spider, and even Donna and Lisa. But instead of receiving what he had hoped for—their encouraging go-get-him-tiger looks—

all Andy received for his query was a sea of uncertain faces bobbing around in an ocean of bewilderment.

Suddenly Lawrence Harris's cheeks puffed visibly pink as he stuck his hands on his hips and his chin defiantly upward and out. "Now you just wait one damn minute, Frank whoever-you-are Montgomery!" A camera started snapping *whizz-click, whizz-click.* "If you, for one minute, think you're going to stand there and soil the reputation of a fine young man like my son here, then you're going to have another thing a-coming!"

"Oh, no, sir," an innocent-looking Frank protested, looking directly at the elder Harris. "You all still don't understand, do you? I'm not here to hurt your handsome son. I'm only here to tell him—to show him and to show you all that he's safe, safe now and forever because he must never for a moment fear exposure from me. Andy, watch this!" Frank showed off the familiar juvenile scrawl with the oversized A. H. in the corner on the envelope that was postmarked "Rachetville" and addressed to Frank Montgomery.

As an obviously confused Mrs. Harris stared for a time at the handwriting she knew so well, she at last turned to Andy and tried to form the question she was almost too frightened to ask. "Well, tell me, son, why . . . why would you write to *him*?"

"It's a trick," screamed Andy. "Can't you see?! Can't you all tell?"

Frank smiled his most engaging smile. "Hey! Hey! No sweat, like I promsied you: Nobody will ever see these letters! Watch this!" Then bending down on one knee before Andy's polished tassled loafers, Frank constructed a pile of the letters before dousing them with lighter fluid and tossing on a burning match. As the pile ignited, there was a chorus of audible gasps from the onlookers. "There! There!" said Frank, staring with immense satisfaction at the conflagration at their feet. "Now you see them," he said, showing for the first time his perfect set of strong white teeth, "and now you don't! And so you, Andy, are safe because the proof of your affair with Stephan Jones is no more."

"You stop all your lying!" shrieked Andy, his voice rising to an octave that nobody would ever mistake as masculine. "You hear me? You better stop those lies right now!" The acknowledged leader of the Rachetville Five sought his father's and mother's eyes for understanding and guidance, but the only thing he received was the same racking confusion that was, even now, visibly overwhelming them.

With the fluid motion of an athlete, Frank Montgomery rose from his bended-knee position to stand straight and proud in front of the stunned gathering, which seemed to be growing by the moment due to fresh infusions of curiosity, mostly from members of the press.

Frank stomped down what remained of the burning ashes. "Well, you can rest easy now, gorgeous guy," he advised Andy before telegraphing him a sly wink and a blown, yet seductive, kiss. "Because what evidence there was has been destroyed."

Frank turned smartly on his heel and began to walk away, but not before Andy began racing after him, arms outstretched, pleading, "Boy, you'd better come back here and tell the truth, you hear? 'Cause what you're doing isn't fair! Please, Frank, please 'cause it's NOT fair!" squawked Andy Harris. "Now, you know, you know, it isn't fair!"

But the only response Andy heard was the chorus of *whizz-click, whizz-click, whizz-click* from the small army of Nikons and the soft hum of the video cameras.

About the Author

BETTE GREENE, who is celebrated for the strong, emotional response that readers have to her books was born in a small Arkansas town. Later she moved to Memphis, Tennessee, and Paris. She now lives in Brookline, Massachusetts with her husband.

Her first novel, *Summer of My German Soldier*, an ALA Notable book, a National Book Award finalist, and a 1973 *New York Times* Outstanding Book of the Year has become a modern classic. Her other novels are: *Philip Hall Likes Me, I Reckon Maybe*, a 1975 Newbery Honor book and a 1974 *New York Times* Outstanding Book of the Year; *Morning Is a Long Time Coming*, the companion volume to *Summer of My German Soldier* and published in 1978; *Them That Glitter and Them That Don't*; and *Get on Out of Here, Philip Hall*.